JUST RIGHT Jillian

JUST RIGHT

Jillian

BY NICOLE D. COLLIER

Versify

An Imprint of HarperCollins*Publishers*

Boston   New York

Versify® is an imprint of HarperCollins Publishers. Versify is a registered trademark of HarperCollins Publishers LLC.

Just Right Jillian

clarionbooks.com

Library of Congress Cataloging-in-Publication Data has been applied for.
ISBN 9780358434610

The text was set in Dante MT Std.
Cover and interior design by Mary Claire Cruz

Manufactured in the United States of America
1 2021
4500843575

First Edition

For Vic

Last Man Standing

It's all Rashida's fault.

Well, my Mama says don't say that. "Never start a story with the other person," she says. But sometimes you *gotta* start with the other person to tell the story. Only this is not a *story* story. It's the truth.

Mama teaches women's leadership workshops. She says leaders look inside, so my problem isn't really with anyone "out there." She makes you point at your imaginary problem, then she makes a big deal about your other three fingers pointing back at *you*.

I don't know about any of that, but I do know my problem is totally Rashida. She's my Foe, with a capital *F*. A foe is your opponent. Or your enemy. I'm not sure we're enemies, but it feels that way some days.

Most days.

Rashida's the smartest person in our school. Even smarter than some teachers, I bet. We were both in Mr. Gray's fourth grade class last year, when Rashida was new to Jemison Elementary.

Everyone thinks she's all that. She speaks "crisply," as Mama would say. She pronounces all her letters, that kinda thing. Her long black twists are thick and shiny—no frizzes flying around. Her sister, Valerie, is like her twin, even though Valerie is a year younger. They dress alike, wearing skirts in invisible colors like beige, tan, blue, or gray. And it's not just them. All the girls blend in with each other. It's not a school uniform or a rule. Boring is just what's in these days, I guess. We all wear ponytails and colors that make you yawn. Unless you wanna stick out like a sore thumb, you just go with the flow. Rashida and Valerie *are* the flow.

They have smooth cocoa brown skin. No freckles. No zits. No braces. No glasses. Nothing. They are perfect. A matching set, tall and graceful.

On the other hand, there's me. I have a small gap in my two front teeth and little moles on my cheeks. Beige makes me want to vomit, but I wear it like everyone else.

Rashida glides everywhere. I run. Across the field. Down the hall. Around the bases. Each day, my black-brown hair is frazzled and dusty by the end of recess. And Daddy tells me to stop swallowing my letters. Only he hears it as "swallowin'." No *g*.

So that's Rashida, and I guess me, too. And now we're in fifth grade.

Ms. Warren (Ms. W. or Ms. Dub for short) is our teacher this year. And she's different. She's younger, like a big sister or a cool auntie. But in some ways she seems older, wise like my Grammy Ruby. She wears her hair cut low, almost bald. And she always has supercool earrings. She looks like a model. She's fun, but she doesn't take any foolishness from kids or anyone else.

She wears these round glasses. They're gold! Have you have ever seen a teacher wear gold glasses? They sparkle, and she can see everything when she puts them on. Everything and everyone, me included. Even though—if I'm being honest—sometimes I don't want anyone to see me at all.

Today we played a math game. Sometimes Ms. W. makes us work on "speed and accuracy" with class competitions. Today's game was Last Man Standing. We should make up a new name because there's no men in our class. Just boys, girls, and Scottie, who doesn't like to be called either one. Here's how the game works:

1. Ms. W. pulls two names from her cup.
2. She calls out a math problem. Easy at first, but they get harder as we go.
3. Whoever's quickest *and* accurate wins the round. Their name goes back into play. The other person is out.

Everyone keeps working on the problems "just for fun" as Ms. W. goes to the next two people.

She goes pair by pair at random until it's the last two. The winner of that round is the last man standing, and she wins the whole thing.

So we played, and finally it was down to us. Me vs. Rashida. My Sworn Enemy. Foe. Or whatever. Guess what happened?

I won.

I. Beat. Rashida.

I finished working the problem while she scribbled the answer. I laid my purple pen on the desk with no fanfare. I floated my hands to the corners of the desk while everyone watched.

But they weren't watching me, they were watching her. Because they knew *she* was going to win. Ms. W. hovered halfway between us, her eyes on Rashida, too.

I listened as Rashida's perfectly sharpened Ticonderoga pencil scratched across her paper. As usual, I kept my face down, kept my mouth shut. I did not put my hand up. I did not yell *DONE!* I did not do a single thing but grip my desk and disappear. I became invisible.

Like my skirt. Like my desk. Beige.

Seconds ticked by like hours, and finally my Foe, my opponent, Rashida, slammed her pencil down in relief as she yelled "DONE!" Loud and proud. Just like I should have. Or could have, but didn't.

I looked up to see what I already knew was true. Ms. W. peered over her golden glasses, checked Rashida's work, and nodded. "You got it! You win!"

The winner gets chocolate. Not just one of the itty-bitty minis. Ms. W. gives out fun-sized! Rashida reached into the huge bag of assorted treats and noisily swirled them around. She yanked out a Snickers, tore it open, and chomped the end.

"Yum!" she yelled in delight. "The sweet taste of victory!" She even flicked her gleaming ponytail.

There was no such joy for me. No flick of the hair. No chomping on my chosen treat. No crunchy milk chocolate and caramel swirls. Instead, my throat was thick with envy.

I couldn't swallow the lump.

My classmates whispered and giggled as they put away their papers and began packing their bags. Ms. W. swept her eyes to me now. I pretended not to notice as I packed up my things. Before the last bell rang, she slid over to me and looked down. First at me, then at my paper. She saw the truth. The real truth.

My correct answer. My silence.

She made a noise that only I could hear. *Hem.* I tugged my ponytail, a twist, low and on the left like every other girl in fifth grade. She waited, and I let my eyes float up to meet her gaze. She pulled off her glasses, and her deep brown eyes asked me why. Why didn't I challenge Rashida after I promised myself I would? Why didn't I speak up? My eyes revealed nothing. They did not answer back. Instead I blinked and looked away.

The bell announced the end of school. I wouldn't have to explain myself this time.

And what would I say? I let Rashida win because I am too shy. I won, but to everyone else, me mostly, I lost. Again.

Ms. W. dismissed us, and I rushed to the bus.

CHAPTER TWO

Tomorrow I Will Be Brave

I held it in until I got all the way home. I remained silent the ten minutes on the bus even though I wanted to yell at myself. Or cry. But I never cry in public, so silence won.

"Man, yo mama feet so crusty . . ." Marquez started today's round of yo mama jokes. Without missing a beat, he caught the paper plane Shelby sailed in his direction. I stared out the window, silently urging Ms. Sally to drive the bus faster.

I clamped my mouth shut so I wouldn't grind my teeth. Did you know that biting the back sides of your tongue is the best way to keep your mouth still? Mama taught me that.

I jumped off first at my stop. Janice and William followed next, whispering to each other. I'm sure I heard the word *lose* drift my way, but I pretended not to notice. The bus pulled off, and I waved goodbye to everyone. Or I tried to, anyway. It was more the helpless flap of a bird's broken wing.

I turned and speed-walked up the hill and around the curve to home, racing to beat the tears. I couldn't even enjoy the dogwoods blooming or the cloudless blue April sky. I wanted to run, to fly away. But I had to look normal.

I breathed through my nose and relaxed my face to erase the wrinkles in my forehead. Another trick from Mama. Did it work? Could anyone tell how close the tears were now? Still rushing, I straightened my posture, pretending a book sat on top of my head. Maybe they wouldn't see the shame.

I passed Ms. Sandy, the neighborhood grandma, walking to meet Little Lonna at the stop. She looked after all the kids. Sometimes, when she's not there, I grab Lonna's hand and walk with her. I'd forgotten about her today.

I jogged the last bit home and nearly tripped up my front step. My hands, keys, and nerves all jangled. It took two tries to unlock the door and get inside. I sprinted to my room and shut the door. Even though nobody was home, I covered my head with my pillow and cried myself to sleep.

☆

Mama knew something was up when she came home from her workshop and I wasn't munching my way through one of my favorite snacks—celery and cheese or apple slices with peanut butter. She woke me with noisy smooches all over my face.

"What's wrong, Jilly Bean?" She leaned down, tickling my chin. Her thick black hair dangled in small coils around her face. I could see the row of eleven mini moles across her cheeks and underneath her eyes. I liked them on her face.

"You never take naps. Something happen in school today?"

I shook my head.

"I know what you need," she said. Planting a kiss on my nose, she stood up. "Coconut curry always cheers you up. I'll make that for dinner." The thought did cheer me a little, and she smiled when she saw me perk up. But she still couldn't coax it out of me.

"The guys are coming over for band practice. You want to go sing with Daddy for a while?"

I shook my head no. I didn't wanna do anything but go back to sleep.

She wouldn't give up. "You're out there less and less these days," she said. "I remember when I couldn't keep you out of that garage. What gives?"

"I just don't feel like singing today."

She stared at me. I looked away. My eyes landed on the smallest of three baskets of yarn. I wondered if it was dusty.

She sighed. "It's hard to believe time is passing so quickly, huh? It's been almost a year already."

I shrugged. I knew how much time had passed. Grammy, Daddy's mom, died exactly eleven months and one day ago. Last May Day. That day felt more like the beginning of winter than the opening of spring.

Grandma was always her wild woman self. That's how

she put it. When she was around—which was all the time, since she lived with us for a spell before she died—I always felt like me, Jillian. It was okay that I was more quiet than loud.

Grandma was quiet, too, in some ways. But she did her own thing her own way. Burning sage and whispering jokes while pretending she couldn't hear half the time. She convinced almost everyone, even the doctors, that she was hard of hearing. I knew the truth. She could hear just fine. She filtered out the "nonsense," as she called it. Every now and again she told me she couldn't hear me either, but she admitted that she just wanted me to be more confident.

My heart was safe with her. "You'll grow out of shyness, Jilly," she said more than once. "But don't hide! Being shy is one thing. Hiding is something else." I never really knew what she meant by hiding. Until today.

Hiding means you're lying. You know what your heart wants, and you're scared, so you do the opposite. Hiding hurts. A lot.

"You miss her?" Mama asked.

I shrugged again. I do miss her. She would know what to do about Rashida. About me being a loser.

Mama tickled my chin one more time, then nodded toward my table. The one I use, or used to use, for weaving. "Your loom is empty," she said. Then she left. She'd been doing that more often lately. Dropping hints. I used to weave, crochet, knit. Weaving most of all. But not since Grammy died. Nothing since then.

I rolled over and looked at my weaving space. The table, the loom, the baskets of yarn sitting on the floor. It did look kinda empty over there. But maybe the loom *did* have yarn and we just couldn't see it. Maybe the yarn was invisible, like me.

I pushed myself up and walked to the mirror. Pulled on my ponytail and leaned into my reflection. I stared at my brown eyes and my black pupils until my eyes watered, and I blinked.

"Why did you disappear, Jilly?" I asked the girl in the mirror. "Why did you let Rashida beat you again?" I looked at myself a little while longer before I sat back down on the bed.

I'm not sure what I was looking for in that mirror, but I don't think I saw it. At school, I don't think my classmates really see me, either. Maybe no one can. Except Ms. W. She has x-ray vision. What I wanna know is, does she see a winner or a loser? Or something in between?

I reached for my bag. Mama doesn't like me to do homework on the bed, but I hoped she wouldn't say anything this time. I was supposed to be thinking about life cycles and chickens hatching, but all I could think about was today. The moment I lost. When I knew the answer, but didn't say. When I shrunk myself into a tiny ball and hid.

How do you stop yourself from disappearing? Do you

wear something special? Do you grow out of it and wake up brave? Do you just hope for the best and see what happens?

Maybe tomorrow will be different.

Maybe tomorrow, they will see me.

Maybe tomorrow, I will be brave.

CHAPTER THREE

Purple and Pockets

I fell asleep wondering how to unhide. More than anything else, Grammy wanted me to be myself. To stop worrying about what everyone thought. "You're just right, Jillian. Be more confident in that."

I promised her I'd do it. And I tried! I read books. Asked Mama for help. Learned to stand up straighter and take deep breaths when I got nervous. Then Grammy left. And in a way, I did, too. In twenty-eight days she'll be gone a year, and I got nothing to show for it. Nothing but losing to Rashida and going with the flow.

I wanted to be able to see it for myself. To say, *You're right, Grammy. I'm just right,* when May Day came around again.

I couldn't just hope things would be different. Grammy said hope is not a strategy. She also wore red every day. She'd say, "If I'm not wearing red, Jilly, something's wrong."

Earrings, nail polish, lipstick, socks. A headband, belt, pants, a skirt. Something red. Every single day.

That gave me an idea.

The next morning, I didn't press the snooze button or wait for Mama's knock. I switched off my alarm as soon as it beeped and rolled myself out of bed in the black morning. If I was serious about being brave, I had to look the part.

I headed to the bathroom to get myself ready. I never like brushing my teeth before I eat breakfast, because I have to brush again after, but Mama says I shouldn't come to the table with morning breath. I got back to my room at 6:10, still five minutes ahead of schedule.

I pulled a purple dress from the closet. I wear it on weekends or when we visit relatives, but never to school. I love this dress because it has pockets. Not just on the sides, but everywhere. You can put crystals or stray yarn in the extra pockets. Or fold up notes from people who love you. Basically, you can carry all the things that give you courage. This is definitely a bravery dress.

Plus, it's purple. No one in Jemison Elementary fifth grade wears purple—or anything that would make it into a Skittles bag. As much as I hate drawing attention to myself, I also hate feeling like I have to do what everyone else is doing. Purple is one of my favorite colors. I could imagine Grammy shimmying her approval. That settled it. Today I would not blend in with everyone else. Today I would be Jillian in Purple and Pockets.

I unbuttoned the pockets on the front to check for the

good stuff. You never know when you might find a dollar to spend or an old piece of gum to chew. No luck. *I'll be cold this morning*, I thought, *but by afternoon the short sleeves'll be just fine.* Georgia Aprils are like that.

I pulled on some white socks. If I wore sneakers instead of sandals, I could play hard during recess. I am so afraid to speak at school. What if I say something weird or stupid? What if I'm wrong and people laugh? But I am never scared during recess. I'm good at running and jumping and hanging upside down and all the things you do outside for fun. These things do not require words or being seen by everyone.

I looked at my hair. Mama lets me do it by myself most of the time now. She fixes it when it doesn't come out quite right, which is most of the time, too. I'm getting better. A little.

It's Tuesday, which means all the girls would have two ponytails instead of one. Hair parted down the middle and braided or twisted. I sprayed my hair with aloe juice to soften it a little and started combing small sections. I'd do mine in four. Two on each side. Double the ponytails. Double the courage.

After five minutes, my four sections were all uneven.

Mama knocked at my door. "Breakfast!" she called.

I grunted and started rushing, and my sections got more uneven. After three tries, my hair was still lopsided and my parts still crooked. I couldn't part a straight line to save my life, and my arms were tired.

"Jillian!" Mama yelled, much sharper now. Her voice squeezed under the closed door and made my heart beat faster.

"You will *not* miss your bus! Breakfast. Now!" Mama opened the door. "What's taking so long?" Her eyebrows rose so high on her face, they disappeared into her hairline. I pointed to the mess on my head.

"I will finish your hair at the table. Let's go."

There's no talking back to Mama. Especially in the morning. Especially when it's almost 6:30 and the bus is coming soon. There was nothing to do but throw everything back into my hair basket and head downstairs.

Daddy handed me a plate of scrambled cheese eggs and toast. He chewed the last bit of his own breakfast before kissing Mama and me and dashing out the door for work. He looks at data — "big data," as he calls it. They're finishing a big project at work, so he's super busy these days.

"I thought I heard you up early," Mama said, softer now. "I'm surprised you're not ready to go."

I ate a forkful of the scrambled clouds. The cheese was still warm and stretchy.

"What were you trying to do with your hair?" Mama asked, already combing through my crooked parts.

"I dunno. I just wanted it in four," I mumbled.

"Let's do four tomorrow, okay? Your middle part is almost perfect. Let's do two." This wasn't a question. Mama lets you solve your own problems until you run out of time, and then she's the Decider in Chief.

She rubbed a little shea butter on her hands to slick my hair so she could pull it into a barrette.

"Don't twist it, please," I said.

"No? You always twist it."

"I just want something different today. Can we leave it loose?"

"Okay," she agreed. She finished the other side, and I finished my eggs and toast.

I reached up and twirled the loose ponytails. Not exactly what I wanted, but they'd have to do. It was 6:35. I needed to leave soon or I'd miss the bus for sure.

Mama smiled at me. "You look pretty." I had on Purple and Pockets, so all was not lost.

"Make it a great day, baby. And don't miss that bus! I have to go get ready."

She pushed me out the door, then leaned over and kissed me goodbye.

Don't Count the Chickens

Shelby saw it first. She is the shortest person in our class, but she makes up for it with her powerful voice. When she shouted "Oh!" clear as day, I heard her even though I was still in the hallway. Had they finally come? We're hatching chicks. The eggs were due to arrive any day now.

Everyone rushed in and crowded around to see. Everyone except me. I lingered behind, not really wanting to be in the middle of everything. I sped up *just a little* and peered into the classroom. Between everyone's heads I could make out an egg incubator sitting on top of the counter. The dome-shaped object was clear on top and yellow on the bottom, with nothing inside.

"It's empty, everyone," called Ms. W. from the board. "I'll explain everything at the right time."

"What time is the right time?" asked William. With his chubby cheeks and long eyelashes, he looked like a doll. But his hazel eyes and soft voice no longer fooled me. William is mean.

"Later," said Ms. W., dry and firm, eyes unblinking.

That was our cue. No more standing around and pointing at things. It was time to get unpacked and ready for the day.

William cut his eyes over to me, inspected my Purple and Pockets, and grunted. A couple of other classmates noticed, too. One girl made a big deal of shielding her eyes, as if attacked by a bright light. Her friend glanced my way and giggled.

I got my school supplies and hung my backpack on my assigned hook. I pulled my shoulders back and walked to my seat with burning cheeks, trying to ignore the attention. "Purple? Bold choice," said Rashida as I passed her and sat down.

I took a deep breath, squinted to make out Ms. W.'s writing on the board, and got to work on the brainteaser.

We didn't have to wait much longer for "later." Once the school announcements were over and we had finally settled down, Ms. W. broke into the quiet.

"It's hatching season." She spoke softly at first, sharing a secret for our ears only. Ms. W. always whispered when she really wanted our attention. And it always worked. We all leaned forward to listen.

"The eggs will arrive after school today and will already be warm and snuggly in the incubator by the time y'all are back tomorrow." She spoke at full volume now, her deep voice, steady and melodic, like an empty glass jar. You know when you wet your fingers and trace the rim? She sounds like that. Daddy calls it contralto.

Ms. W. said we would learn something new each day, and in twenty-one days, if all goes well, the eggs will hatch. We have to take notes in a regular journal, with pencil and paper.

"Writing is an important tool of scientists," she announced.

"Ms. W., why do you always have the biggest hatch?" Shelby asked what we all wanted to know. Ms. W. is the champion of the chickens—she's hatched the most for three years running.

"The other teachers say I'm lucky. Either that or I pick the best incubator and leave them with the quirky ones."

I shook my head. That didn't make sense.

"That's not the reason," said Marquez, who was shaking his head, too.

"Maybe it's my big heart," Ms. W. joked, and she explained that she checks on them constantly, making sure they are the right temperature and everything.

"But don't the other teachers care? Don't they check the temperature and all that, too?" Shelby asked.

"Yes, but they've been at it a lot longer than I have. Ten or fifteen years."

We didn't see the connection, but Ms. W. explained that you have to be careful not to take things for granted. If you assume things will go well just because they always have, you may be in for an unhappy surprise.

"How many chickens are coming?" asked Marquez.

I think this struck a nerve. Instead of her usual calm stillness, her eyes grew round and her hands waved like flags in high wind.

"They are *not* chickens," she said. "They are *eggs!* And if all conditions are right, they will *grow* into chickens. But sometimes things just happen. There's a reason for the saying 'Don't count your chickens before they hatch.'"

She wrote this last part on the board in big block letters.

DON'T COUNT YOUR CHICKENS BEFORE THEY HATCH

She even made us say it out loud while she pointed to each word.

"Don't. Count. Your. Chickens. Before. They. Hatch!" we yelled in unison.

"It's true for all of us," she said. "Anyone can fail to develop if conditions aren't right. We do what we can, and we wait and see."

"How many, though?" Marquez asked again. He jokes around a lot, but he doesn't miss much.

"Oh, right. I'm not sure," said Ms. W. "Maybe ten? I won't know until they arrive."

Shelby wouldn't let her question go either. "Don't the other teachers love the chick—I mean eggs, too?"

Ms. W. nodded.

"Then what's the difference?" Rashida asked, her hand on her chin. She looked like a small grownup, her legs crossed and everything. I couldn't tell if she was being snippy or curious.

"Maybe they're right." Ms. W. shrugged. "Maybe it's luck."

I know better. Ms. W. hatches more chicks because she sees them. She can look through the eggs with her golden glasses and her x-ray vision and see the truth inside.

⭐

On the bus ride home I looked out the window, clenching my jaws.

"I thought only little kids dressed like crayons!"

"Nah, today was violet day. She gonna wear indigo tomorrow—like a rainbow."

I pretended I couldn't hear them. But I always hear them. I shifted my bookbag to cover a few more inches of me. Pressed myself deeper into the seat. Soon enough, the snarky voices began gossiping about other people.

I thought more about Ms. W., wondering if my parents had x-ray vision, too. Could they see the inside of me? Maybe if they could see me better, Mama could give me better hints on what to do. How to stop hiding. How to stop worrying about what other people think.

Mama was there when I got home. I found her in the kitchen, humming and dancing to Pharrell's song "Happy," with an ink pen sticking in her hair. She calls it her deep-thinking ritual.

"Welcome home, Jilly Bean!" she said, greeting me with a kiss on my forehead. "I got your snack ready." She pointed to the counter. "I'm on a roll with this new workshop, so I'm gonna work a little more before knocking off for the day. Okey-dokey?"

"Dokey-okey," I said.

"School okay?" she asked over her shoulder.

"Yeah," I said, glad she was distracted so I could skip over the bad parts. "Guess what?"

She turned back to me, waiting for more.

"We're getting eggs tomorrow. We're hatching chickens."

"Oh, that's right! They will be so cute. And look who's smiling? You were so down yesterday."

I shoved a cheese-covered celery into my mouth and nodded while I chomped. Her eyes searched my face for other clues. I guess nothing grabbed her attention, because her eyes glazed over the way they always do when she's in a creative zone. She pivoted to leave, but I had to ask my question.

"Mama?"

She turned back again. "Jilly?"

"What do you see when you see me?" I tried to make my voice sound like no big deal. Like, *What do you see when you look out the window?*

She paused, her eyes tuning back in, looking more closely now. Concerned.

"I see my smart and beautiful daughter," she said.

"And Daddy?" I asked quietly.

"I'm sure he sees what I see. Why are you asking? What do *you* see?"

"I don't know." I stared at the next stalk of celery.

She paused again. "Is someone bothering you at school, Jilly?" She stepped closer, ready to get the truth out.

"No," I said. *Rashida's being Rashida. William's being William. I'm letting Grammy down.*

"What do you *want* to see?" she asked.

I twirled my hair. "Me."

She took a deep breath, nodding as she exhaled.

"Well, Jilly, the good news is, you're always there, honey. You are a creative thinker, a talented weaver, a lovely singer and energetic performer, a caring friend. You are many things, and all of them are you."

Maybe I was some of those things — when Grammy was still here.

Mama grabbed my face. "Are you sure there's no one bothering you at school? Or something you need to tell me?"

"Yeah."

She stared at me. If she were an emoji, it would be called "unconvinced face."

"I'm sure."

She stared some more, and then it was my turn to take a deep breath. A slow, quiet relaxing one just the way she taught me. She giggled, noticing.

"Okay." She sounded unsure, but kissed me again, this time on the nose. "I love you, don't forget," she said.

"I won't." I put another piece of celery into my mouth as she disappeared into her office.

I chomped the celery and chewed on the questions swirling in my head. She said I am always there, but who am I, really? Who is Jillian? And why can't I see her for myself?

☆

When Daddy finally got home, he came to kiss me good night. My room was dark, except for the light floating in from the hallway. Even in the shadows, I could tell his long locks were pulled back in a "professional" ponytail.

"So what's this I hear about you being down after school today?"

I hoped he couldn't see my cheeks burning. I shrugged in the dark. I didn't really have anything to say.

"Well, I have known you from the day you were born until now. Did you know that's about" —he paused— "five million minutes?"

"Really?"

"Really! But I don't need five million data points to know you're awesome."

I giggled.

"Okay?" he asked.

"Okay."

He found my nose and kissed it good night.

CHAPTER FIVE
Playing the Dozens

A chorus of "oooh, aaahh" spilled out into the hallway just as I got to the classroom. I skipped inside and saw what all the fuss was about—the incubator was filled with white eggs!

There was a counting match, and after a few trip-ups, we agreed there were twelve. Ms. W. stood back, her arms folded, laughing at us. "Yes, twelve," she confirmed.

Marquez broke into a big smile then, his braces gleaming bright. He grabbed a black pencil from a nearby desk and held it up to his mouth like a microphone. He cleared his throat and introduced the eggs to the crowd:

"Welcome to the stage, Cheaper by the Dozen!

"Let's give a warm welcome to The Baker's Dozen. Wait, no, The Dirty Dozen!

"You know it's time for fun when you hear, 'Let's play the dozens—'"

We laughed and clapped, but it all faded out when we caught sight of Ms. W. throwing one of her burning looks.

You don't want her eyes drilling into you like that. You feel like a pile of crispy leaves set on fire by a big match. *Whoosh!* Up you go in smoke.

We froze, but Marquez, he smiled, flexing his dimple, cool as you please.

"Come on Ms. W.," he teased, "you know it was funny."

We snickered behind our hands, shielding ourselves from her glare. She shook her head at first, but she broke, and the smile came easing from her lips. A smile followed by a sigh.

"I'm warning you," she said. "Do not get attached. Do not count your chickens—"

"BEFORE THEY HATCH!" we all yelled.

She sighed again. "By the way, a baker's dozen is thirteen, not twelve," she teased Marquez.

"Ohhhhh," we all ribbed, laughing.

"I see you, Ms. Dub, I see you. I fixed it, though. Dirty. Dirty Dozen." Marquez laughed.

Most of the time, science is at the end of the day, but Ms. W. said she could tell we wouldn't get anything else done until we discussed those eggs. After all the giggles, she drew an arrow on the day's agenda, flip-flopping math and science. We all clapped and hooted.

"You still need to do your morning work," she called out over the noise. Today's assignment was a writing prompt. We had to write what we knew about chickens and what we wanted to learn during the unit.

She also reminded us about our journals. Each day we were supposed to document and respond to what's happening inside the egg—or "life inside the oval," as she called it. We can't just draw and caption. We have to be thoughtful. Ms. W. likes us to *connect* with our learning. She says that makes us more well-rounded humans.

That means answering questions, like

What do you think?

What do you wonder?

What do you hope?

A few kids groaned, but I don't mind journals. I'm always thinking, wondering, and hoping about something. And it's way safer to think or write stuff like that instead of saying it out loud. For one, I think chickens are cool, even though I've never seen one in person. I used to wonder which came first? The chicken or the egg? But I really wanna know what it feels like to change from an egg into a chicken. Does it feel like anything? Does it hurt?

☆

"You may not have realized this, but watch." Ms. W. pressed play on a video. "The mother hen turns her eggs every so often. See?"

"Is that what they're doing? Why?" asked Jake. In a sea of brown faces, Jake's one of the few white kids at Jemison. He's also the tallest kid in class, so he really stands out.

"A few reasons, and we'll talk about them later on. One is

to help keep the egg temperature even. For us, the incubator will do that."

"What's another one?" Scottie wondered.

"Well, so the embryo doesn't get stuck to the egg membrane."

"Yuck! Gross!" Everybody pretended to gag.

"Like I said, we'll learn about this as we go. But our incubator will do the turning. So if you hear a motorized sound or see a small movement, that's what's happening. Whatever you do, be careful. Don't slam your books on the counter or throw things near the incubator. Got it?"

We all nodded, agreeing to Ms. W.'s terms of good behavior.

Then she switched to a photo. Imagine if someone took an egg and sliced it in half the long way—from the oval tip to the round butt. That's how it looked. She called it the cross section.

"What do you notice about this egg?" she asked.

To be honest, no one noticed anything at first. But Ms. W. is famous for her Wait Time. She will just ask a question and wait. If you could see Wait Time, it would look like a blank sheet of paper.

She just waits silently until someone answers.

The first time she tried Wait Time with our class, we all giggled because it was so weird. But she explained that sometimes we need to be okay with silence. That we need silence to think. She's right. Grammy always said she needed quiet to hear herself think. She even taught me to weave with no music or TV or anything. Today Ms. W. posted that picture and waited until someone had an answer.

Rashida spoke up first, of course. "What's that white dot?" she asked.

I squinted while everyone started to say things like "Oh yeah" and "I see it, right there." Finally I could make it out.

"If all conditions are right, that is a future chick. That little spot is called a blastoderm," said Ms. W. as she wrote it on the board.

"*Blast off!*" shouted Marquez. Everyone laughed.

"Settle down, please," Ms. W. warned. "But you're right, in a way."

Marquez leaned back in his chair, nodding like a king on his throne. I rolled my eyes at him. He licked his tongue out at me, then smiled, his braces flashing.

Ms. W. ignored him.

She explained that today is officially day one of about twenty-one days. The future chick is a bunch of cells—the blastoderm or the bull's-eye. There's not much to see yet, but apparently lots of stuff is happening.

She put up another picture, zooming in a bit. We drew what we saw and labeled the pieces in our journals—shell, membrane, albumen, yolk, and bull's-eye.

Then we partnered up with other kids nearby. Shelby

picked Janice, as usual, so that left me and Marquez to work together.

Ms. W. came around with an egg carton and small bowls. We all took a raw egg and broke it open. I was scared to think we were killing chickens—embryos—by cracking them open. I think she figured we were all a little creeped out because she said, "Don't worry, these are regular unfertilized eggs. They weren't going to grow into anything." *Except maybe an omelet,* I thought. But then I felt creeped out all over again.

As we studied our raw eggs, Ms. W. reminded us that the albumen is the egg white.

"Right!" said Jake. "My mom eats those when she's on a diet."

"I object!" yelled Shelby, jumping out of her seat. We all froze and stared at her squinchy face. She looked like she might cry any second. "Can we not discuss eating animals, please? Everyone knows I'm vegan." She folded her arms across her chest.

I don't know if everyone knew, but I didn't. I guess we all know now. I felt really glad I didn't say the omelet thing out loud.

Ms. W. called Shelby over for one of her "private chats." That's when she wants to tell you something "for your own good," but she will keep it quiet to save face. I colored in my sketch while stealing looks at Shelby and Ms. W. Whatever they said, Shelby just nodded. She came back to her seat with her face a little less squinchy.

I thought about Shelby all day after that. She was upset and said so. She spoke up and didn't hesitate at all. I wonder how she got to be so brave. Did someone teach her, or did she figure it out on her own? Does she wear special barrettes or socks? Maybe she skips the worrying part and gets straight to saying what's on her mind. Maybe one day I can do that, too.

CHAPTER SIX

The Invitation

Some schools have spelling bees. Others have MATH-COUNTS competitions or geography bees. We have the Jemison Mind Bender, and April is Mind Bender season. Baby blue Mind Bender flyers covered the walls when we walked into school the next day.

It's sort of a big deal, but Mind Bender is really a big trick. We don't have those scary standardized tests in May anymore. The teachers wanted a fun way to get us to review the stuff we've learned all year, so someone came up with Mind Bender.

Every grade level has questions for every subject. But there are also challenge questions, trivia or stuff you would learn in later grades. If you can answer those, you get extra points. You play in rounds.

Mind Bender Rounds

Practice: Just what it sounds like. It doesn't count yet.

Prelims: Play with your classmates. The top two players in every *class* advance.

Round 1: Play against the other class winners in your grade level. The top five players in every *grade* advance.

Round 2: Things get tough here. Only the top two winners from every grade level advance to the finals.

Finals: There's the Big League for older kids and Little League for younger. The Big League winner is the Mind Bender champion.

Every year a second-grader wins the Little League Mind Bender and a fifth-grader wins the Big League one. No surprise, right? It's always that way. At least it always *was* that way.

Last year, a fourth-grader won Jemison Elementary's Big League Mind Bender for the first time. You know who that fourth-grader was?

Rashida. Who else?

☆

So I saw the flyers this morning (who didn't?), but I ignored them. There's just no way I'd make myself compete in front of everybody and they mama. If I got the answers wrong, folks would think I was dumb. If I got them right, the audience would get bigger every round. No ma'am. Not my idea of fun.

It's like the Last Person Standing. I usually know the answer, but I can only make myself blurt it out half the time. *I hate being put on the spot.* That was my last thought when I walked into class and felt, then saw, Ms. W.'s eyes on me.

She talks with her eyes just as much as her mouth. When she gives you The Look, with a capital *L,* you know you'd better be quiet or else! Sometimes it's an invitation. She wants you to say more, so she raises her eyebrows and makes her eyes smile.

Earlier this week she gave me a look that said *Oh, that's interesting,* when I was/wasn't the Last Person Standing. That's how I knew she saw me. The truth. But today when I walked into class, she gave me a look I couldn't read.

I felt myself blending, trying to hide from whatever it was. But she went on with class as usual. Maybe I was wrong. Maybe she didn't look at me strange after all.

When we lined up for lunch, Ms. W. tapped me on the shoulder and said she wanted to talk to me. I guess I looked nervous. She told me to stop frowning, so I wouldn't get the wrong wrinkles. "The right wrinkles come from laugh lines, you know," she said. But I felt frowning was the right thing to do for now. Ms. W. signaled to Scottie, today's line leader, to head out to the cafeteria. I was the caboose of the line. Last.

"Stop slouching," she whispered as we began to move. "There's nothing to hide from."

I didn't agree. Hiding from the unknown is how you stay safe. You come out again when the danger is gone. But I didn't say anything. Instead, I imagined a big dictionary on my head. I read about it in a modeling book last year. If you want to look more confident, walk around balancing a big book on your head. It makes you stand up straight. I stood taller and pulled my shoulders back. As soon as most of the class got their trays and milk and picked seats, Ms. W. and I went over to the corner to talk.

"I want you to do the Mind Bender." She whipped out one of the baby blue flyers and waved it in my direction. "The practice round is tomorrow. The official competition begins next week."

I knew without her saying it that I scrunched up my face again. Mama always said I needed to work on poise. You're poised when you're calm, cool, and collected under pressure. Slouching and balling up your face when something is scary means you're probably not calm, or cool, or collected. It means you're not confident. I wasn't.

Mama thinks if you act confident, you'll feel confident. So far, walking tall hasn't done a thing to help me feel better. It just gives me better posture.

Face still scrunched, I didn't say anything. Ms. W. didn't either. I had no hopes of beating the inventor of Wait Time, so I broke first. "What if I don't want to do that?"

"Which part?" she asked. "Practice for the Mind Bender or win it?"

Now things were getting out of hand. *Win?* I thought. *She's really out there.*

"Stop looking like you smell something, Jillian. Answer me. Do you want to practice? Do you want to win?" My heart fluttered at the thought—the hope—of the yes. There was no way I'd say it out loud.

"Everyone knows who the winner will be," I mumbled.

"Do they?" she asked, shooting her laser beams at me.

I shook my head in disbelief. Ms. W. knew the story! Rashida won last year. As a fourth-grader, she beat everyone in school. We're in fifth grade now, so . . . It seemed obvious to me. Ms. W. told me to think about it. And if I didn't like the practice, I didn't have to compete. She thought it would be "good for me." That's what your parents say when they want you to try roasted eggplant or Brussels sprouts. I didn't want anything good for me. I just wanted to disappear.

"Think about it," she said again, locking her eyes on mine. I blushed, remembering I was supposed to be brave this week.

"Yes, ma'am," I said, barely moving my lips.

I trudged over to our table and squeezed in beside Marquez and Shelby. I looked up, surprised to be almost eye to eye with Rashida. She sat across from me, when usually she sat much farther away. She gave a look, almost like a wink, but that would've been strange. *Is she in on it? Does she know what Ms. W. just asked?* I wondered.

I ate my cold tuna melt in silence while Marquez tried to tell me about his sister. I have no idea what he said. I think I muted him in my mind. I just wanted to go home and "think about it" in peace.

✩

Today is day two of life inside the oval.

The eggs have to stay in the incubator the whole time they are developing. They need to be the right temperature, too. Close to 100 degrees. That seems too hot to me. Like two p.m. in late July, but all day for two weeks straight. But Ms. W. reminded us that our body temperature is pretty close to that, so it's not as hot as it seems.

She flashed a picture of what it looks like inside the egg today, but as far as I could tell by squinting, it was basically the same as yesterday. Except for one thing.

Today's egg sketch included a small spot for blood vessels. Later in the day they will form a heart, and soon after that, it will beat!

How can that be possible? It's just an egg. An egg with a beating heart? And so soon!

If it has a heartbeat, can it get nervous?

Like I feel my heart beating when I'm afraid.

Like my heart fluttered when Ms. W. asked me about Mind Bender.

Like the pounding when I won/lost the Last Person Standing.

When I am not sure what to do, when I am nervous, it beats so strong, drumming my voice into silence.

CHAPTER SEVEN
Egg on Your Face

At recess the next day, Ms. W. had the practicing Mind Benders sit on the curb. I took a deep breath and joined Rashida, Shelby, Jake, and Marquez. Marquez said he came because he thought it would be fun. Fun? Hearing that only made me more nervous.

Everyone else was all smiles. Even Shelby, though her mom was making her do the Mind Bender. Why was I there, when I could be somewhere running or hanging upside down? *Because I'm smart,* I answered myself. *Because hiding hurts. Because I promised Grammy I'd learn to believe in myself.*

We all sat at attention. Ms. W. pushed her sparkly spectacles up her nose and swiped a few times on her tablet.

"Okay, everyone. The topics and questions will be selected at random. Time is important. Answer as fast as you can. Got it?"

"Got it!" said everyone else. I wasn't so sure.

She warmed us up by asking each of us a question. She started with Rashida and went on down the line. Every time someone went, my heart beat harder, faster. Waiting was the worst.

Then it was my turn. When she asked my question— what is a simple machine?—I just looked down at my knees, wondering if Marquez could feel my heart beat, too.

"Jillian, this is a timed competition?" Ms. W.'s voice slid upward into a question, asking me to hurry. I looked up and saw her eyebrows reaching for the sky. Waiting.

I nodded and swallowed hard.

"Do you know the answer?" she asked.

"I dunno." Everyone turned and looked at me, confused. Rashida, the farthest away, leaned forward to register her surprise, too. I felt my armpits prickle. I squeezed my elbows to my waist just in case I started to sweat.

"You don't . . . know if you know?" asked Jake.

"I mean, I do, but . . ."

"But what?" Ms. W. did that thing where adults get mad but try to act like they aren't mad. If I didn't say something, she'd probably just ask me again.

"But I don't think my answer is the answer you want."

"Try me," she said.

I mumbled about a tool applying a force, like a lever or a pulley.

"Why didn't you say that in the first place?" she asked.

"I didn't think it would count."

"The answer?" Marquez asked, looking really confused now.

"*My* answer," I said.

"Well—there's only one right answer, right?" asked Shelby.

I tried to explain. "That's just it, sometimes my answers are *different*—"

"But if it was *different*," said Jake, "wouldn't it be *wrong*?"

My cheeks burned. "People always think different means wrong." I said this more to the curb than to anyone else.

Like the Coriolis effect, I thought. Last year we learned about weather events. At the end of the unit, my teacher asked us to share something we learned. He put me on the spot. No warning or anything, I had to go first. At home I'd read about the Coriolis effect—in the Southern Hemisphere, hurricanes spin in the opposite direction from the way they spin here. With all those eyes on me, I couldn't remember what it was called.

I stuttered and stammered while he kept asking me to explain what I meant when I said, "Sometimes hurricanes go backwards." Everyone laughed. I cried inside. William, who has been in all my classes since first grade, called me

Hurricane Girl for weeks. It wasn't the first time I had trouble explaining something I knew, but it was the last time I tried.

"But sometimes there is only one right answer," Jake insisted.

"Sometimes," I said under my breath, ready to give up.

"Well, if your answer is just different, why can't you explain it?" Rashida asked—like *duh!* Maybe she didn't mean to make me feel stupid, but I did.

I slouched then, embarrassed. I bit the back of my tongue. No teeth grinding. No tears. Neutral face. Mama's suggestions don't help me feel more confident, but they do keep me from making a fool of myself.

"Relax, Jillian," said Ms. W. "Whatever answer comes to mind, just say it. Don't worry if it matches what I think. Okay?"

I nodded to my knees.

She spoke to everyone now. "These are free-for-alls. There are five of you and twenty-one questions. Whoever has the most correct answers, wins. I'm keeping score."

She straightened her glasses, swiped her tablet, and cleared her throat to begin. Every question she asked, I knew the answer. Sometimes a second or so too late, and sometimes before everyone else spoke. But no one knew the difference. I only answered them in my head. Never out loud. I tried to speak, I really did. But every time, the words got stuck between my head and my mouth. At first I was nervous. I just didn't want to say the wrong thing. Then I was embarrassed because it looked like I didn't know *anything*. Either way, my mouth stayed shut.

By the end I stopped trying to force the words out. I just nodded and listened and checked off the right answers inside my head.

The practice round took the whole recess. Rashida won, and Marquez got runner-up. Ms. W. signaled that it was time to go, and everyone started back inside. I dragged my feet so I could be last. Alone.

It didn't work, because soon Rashida walked up to me.

"You knew all those answers, didn't you?" she asked so only I could hear.

I nodded, surprised she asked me something like that. Or anything.

She nodded back, but didn't say anything else. She rushed ahead, catching up with the class, and Marquez hung back with me.

"So . . . what's up?" he asked.

"They want you to be mind readers," I complained, trying to defend myself.

"They want to know what you think. Or know. They want you to be accurate," said Marquez.

"Nobody cares what's in *my* head. If I don't say it *exactly* like it is on that app or whatever, it's wrong!"

He stopped walking then and frowned at me. "You're always like this!"

"Like what?"

"How can you ever know what counts as wrong? You say you got all these ideas, but you never say 'em out loud. Why not?"

"Because." I folded my arms, torn between yelling and crying. But I don't cry in public. Or yell. Nothing to bring attention.

"'Cause what?"

'Cause when thoughts and words and hurricanes spin in the wrong direction, nobody knows what you mean. And everybody thinks you're stupid.

"People only hear what they wanna hear," I protested.

"Well, they can't hear nothing if you don't say nothing."

I pouted, but I didn't argue. We had to catch up, and there was nothing else I could say.

✫

At the end of the day I went to Ms. W. It was time to quit. Smart people know when they're in over their heads. There had to be another way to make good on my promise to Grammy.

Before I could get it out, she shushed me with a finger to her lips. "Think about it," she said. She still believed I should compete in the classroom competition next week. "Ask your parents about it, see what they say."

I could imagine what they'd say: *relax and be yourself.*

"Think about it, Jillian, okay?" she repeated as the dismissal bell rang. "You can do this."

I finished packing my bookbag and dashed to the bus.

I didn't speak to anyone on the ride home, but inside my head it was plenty noisy. I heard chickens clucking. Talking to me like I'm one of them. *Why do we say that people who are afraid of things are chickens, anyway?* I wondered.

I know I can do it. I know I can at least answer the questions. I don't really know why I choke up. I just know it's something inside of me. A mean judge sitting high on a bench, telling me quiet is better. Sit still. Blend in. Be invisible.

So I listen. I'm quiet. I blend in. But it doesn't feel good. Makes my stomach tight. And Mama says your stomach always knows the truth even when your head doesn't.

☆

When I got home, I opened the door to Daddy blasting music from his phone. I think it was a recording of his band. He's in a real band—a rock band!

Sometimes on Fridays he leaves the office at lunchtime. Once in a while he even works from home the whole day. He says his job is fun but stressful. To relax, he plays music with his friends. Their band, Human Revolution, doesn't plan to be famous, but sometimes they play real gigs at clubs around town. Usually they play in our garage. Daddy built a small stage with lights and everything.

He still had on a work polo and jeans, bobbing his head when I walked in.

"There's my girl!" He scooped me up and swung me around. His hair flew around, too. Daddy has long, reddish-brown locks, so he looks like a friendly lion when it's all loose. I'm almost in middle school, but every now and again he likes to prove he's still strong enough to give me a twirl. I giggled in his arms.

"How was school?" he asked, smiling.

I stopped giggling. "It was okay."

He put me down softly. "That good, huh?"

"Yeah."

"I know what'll be fun. Come jam with us! The guys are coming after work. When's the last time you sang with us, Jilly Bean? You have that pretty alto. I'd like to hear more of it."

So would everyone, and me too, I thought. I shook my head no.

"It's Friday! What's on your mind? Any of your friends having a sleepover? You want to invite anyone here?"

"No, Daddy. I'll probably just watch TV or read a book or something."

"Hmm," he said. "Well, if you change your mind about singing with us, just come on out."

I nodded, but I didn't plan to sing. By the time I got to my room, I heard Daddy playing on his keyboard. He's much better on guitar, but he likes to practice. Says that's how you get better at anything, even when you're grown.

When was the last time I sang? Really sang with him or the band? It took a second, but then I could see it, clear as day. Me and Daddy singing one Friday night, Mama and Grammy in the audience, waving their hands in the sky and singing back to us like it was a real concert. Beautiful Mama in perfect harmony and wild woman Grammy singing off key, showing me in her own way it was okay to be yourself.

She had been visiting us more often by then. Staying longer. Daddy worried she spent too much time alone in Savannah, and he insisted she just move in with us. That day, she finally agreed, saying she could "spend more time with my Jillian." We gave her a welcome home concert to celebrate. Now I lay on my bed, remembering, still trying not to cry even though no one was watching.

After Daddy played a few scales, he started "Push" by Lenny Kravitz. That's his favorite warm-up song. I heard his soothing baritone floating up through the house. You know how in cartoons you can always see the trails of the yummy-smelling dessert making their way to someone who isn't supposed to eat it? His voice is like that. Winding through the house, finding my ears.

In my room, I sang along. Tried to, anyway. Then the

words, like all my ideas, got caught in my throat. Stuck between my mind and my mouth. I wasn't too shy or too nervous this time, just too sad. I listened to him singing about making the best of his reality. Singing the words I knew in my heart.

CHAPTER EIGHT
Eyes on the Prize

Mama and I parked in front of the bookstore, 9th Palace. We kept a strict budget so we wouldn't spend too much money there, but we always came away with piles of books. Most Saturdays we went there, then sometimes to Keet's, the craft shop next door, before grocery shopping.

At Keet's I could buy beads and new yarns or even take weaving or jewelry-making lessons. We hadn't been there in ages, but this morning Mama said she wanted me to get some inspiration, get my creative juices flowing again.

"Maybe we can go to the movies later," Mama said, thumbing over her shoulder to the movie theater across the parking lot. "Anything you want to see?"

I squinted. Today's showtimes were posted in black block letters, but it was a blurry mess to me. "I don't know . . . I can't really see that far."

Mama gasped, sounding horrified. "You can't read that?" she shouted at me.

I pressed my eyes and squinted again while she watched, her mouth hanging open. "Now I can." I smiled. "And I can see you."

She wrinkled her forehead and made the "that's not funny" face. Then she asked if I could see at school. I told the truth, which is mostly, yeah. Especially if I'm sitting near the front or squinting.

"Why didn't you say anything?"

I didn't have an answer. I *could* see, mostly. I shrugged.

She sucked in a loud breath and blew it out.

"You're going to the eye doctor," she told me. "I will see if I can get an appointment today since it's still early." She whipped out her phone and scrolled through her contacts.

"You can't go around squinting, Jillian. You need to speak up! Let us know when you need something." She pointed at me now—all her other fingers pointing back at her. I knew better than to say anything about that.

Her optometrist could squeeze me in, but only if we came right away. That settled it. We left the plaza and headed in the other direction.

✫

The eye doctor's office looked like an art studio. We walked in on smooth concrete floors. You could see the bricks and pipes on the inside, which Mama says is "an upgrade." Off to one side sat a Keurig machine and a little metal tree layered with Keurig pods on a marble counter. It was warm outside, but I sort of wanted to make some hot chocolate. Why not? But Mama said no. Which I guess turned out to be fine, since right after that someone called my name.

"Jillian?" A smiling lady with funky lime green boxy glasses and a big, curly bush of hair waved me back. Mama followed us down the hall into a small, dark space. It was more a closet than a room.

"Sit here," said Miss Boxy-Bushy. "We have to measure the pressure in your eyes." I must've frowned up, because she smiled and said, "You just have to hold still and I'll blow a little air. It's a breeze." Mama snickered at the pun as I put my chin and forehead where Miss Boxy-Bushy instructed. I opened my right eye really wide. But then I blinked. And blinked. And blinked again. It was impossible to sit still, just waiting for something to hit my eye.

Then it happened. It was not a breeze but a *puff* of air instead! And because I blinked, she had to do it like seven or seventeen times on the right eye before she finally said, "Got it!"

But then we had to start all over and do the same thing to the left eye. It's true it didn't hurt, but it was still weird. I kept blinking, though maybe I blinked slower or her reflexes got faster. It only took three tries on the left. She laughed the whole time, but I didn't see anything funny. I just wanted it to be over.

Then we went to a bigger room, like when you see the

doctor or dentist. I had to sit in a big chair, like a pilot or something. Mama sat on the side in a regular chair. Before I got a chance to look around, in walked Dr. Benjamin. A dark, towering man with a deep but quiet voice. He had a big, toothy smile and said everything twice—like "Well, well! How are you? How are you?"

He sat down and got right to business, waving lights and mirrors and making me read big, jumbled letters projected on a white wall. I kept blinking, waiting for him to blow air into my eyes. I guess he figured that out because he told me to relax my shoulders and stop gritting my teeth. "You did the hard part," he said. "The rest is easy. The rest is easy."

I'll be the judge of that, I thought. *I'll be the judge of that.*

I leaned into the big metal plates he pressed against my forehead. He flicked down an eye patch to cover my right eye. Then he started asking me questions.

"What's the smallest row you can read without squinting?"

"Does this make it better or worse? Better or worse?"

He'd click something, move a lens across my face, and ask more questions.

"Which is better. One or two? Three or four?"

Sometimes they looked the same, and I felt bad saying I didn't know. I kept wondering if he really knew which one *should* be better and was just waiting for me to get it right.

He would adjust the lens and ask me again in the same soft voice.

"Which is better, five or six? Does this make it better or worse? Better or worse?"

He did the same on both eyes, and then he let me see the jumbled letters without the eye patch.

When it was all over, he announced that I am near-sighted, with astigmatism. It means I need help seeing things far away, and even close up it's not "crisp." It's blurry because of the shape of my eye. "It's not good to push and press on your eyes. Or rub them at all. Or rub them at all," he said. "You want to keep your eyes healthy for the rest of your life! Be nice to them. Be nice."

I nodded, but I would never be mean to my eyes, or anyone or anything.

After he wrote my prescription, Mama and I went to pick out my new glasses. We pretended to be models. I made duck lips and cheesy smiles for selfies, putting on frames and taking them off again. After a parade of frames in all sizes and colors, we found two that Mama and I both liked—brown tortoiseshell frames and some bright red ones. Both small ovals. Mama called them cat eyes. Because they're shaped like, well you know, cat eyes.

"Which ones?" Mama asked. I knew she liked the brown ones better. She kept going on about how they were neutral and versatile. They would blend in and wouldn't clash with anything, and wasn't that great?

But deep down I wanted the red ones. Would they match my school clothes? My personality? I'm not as perky as those glasses. What would people say? They were so bright and cheerful sitting there on the shelf. More than that, they looked brave! They looked poised and confident, not shy. Maybe I would be poised and confident if I wore them.

Plus, red was Grammy's color. Maybe this was the trick. I imagined myself wearing them at school. Being a Mind Bender. Sounding cool and smart, looking the part.

"Today, Jilly," the Decider in Chief warned, interrupting my thoughts. That meant I was running out of time. I took a deep breath. I sort of closed my eyes and pointed. I guess it looked like I wanted the brown ones. Or maybe Mama wanted me to want them, because she said, "We'll take these," holding up the brown frames. Miss Boxy-Bushy looked surprised. "Are you sure?" she asked in Mom's direction. But she really looked at me. I pretended not to see her seeing me. I did what I do best now. I hid.

"Yes," said Mama. While Miss Boxy-Bushy helped Mama figure out the details—no glare, no scratch coating, and all that, I saw the words in my head. *Can we get the red ones instead? I really want the red ones.* But they were stuck inside and wouldn't come out of my mouth.

Just like always.

CHAPTER NINE

Master Your Mind

"You're quiet," Daddy said later on. He came into my room to see what I was up to. The three of us usually hung out on Saturday afternoons, watching TV or playing games. Today I read alone in my room instead.

"Yeah."

"What's on your mind, kiddo?"

"I went to the eye doctor today."

"Yeah. Mama said she caught you squinting. How was it?"

"Fine. I have to get glasses."

"It's not the end of the world. Your mom and I both wore glasses growing up. The kids won't make fun of you too much, will they?"

"They probably won't notice."

He paused for a second. "Why not? Don't you have friends at school?"

I shrugged. What could I say to explain? "Sorta. They talk to me. But they don't see me, not really."

"Do you show yourself to them? Showing up at school is not the same as showing the real you. What do you say?"

I shrugged. "Nothing special."

"It doesn't have to be special. It just has to be you. You're special."

"I don't feel special." I swallowed hard. "I don't feel like anything," I said, whispering now, my face heating up.

"You can't be this down because of the glasses. I'm sure they're fine."

"They're wrong." I felt tears welling up in my eyes, but I tried to hold them in.

"What's wrong, Jilly Bean?" he asked, and just like that, they were free. Tears streamed down my face.

"My glasses. We got the wrong ones . . ." I sobbed. "We got the plain brown ones. They match everything. I want the bright red glasses that don't match."

"You want *red* glasses?"

I nodded, feeling silly for crying about red glasses. But it wasn't just the glasses. It was the Mind Bender. Rashida. I wanted to be brave at school. I wanted to make Grammy proud.

"Well, that's easy to fix, honey. Why didn't you say so?"

I sniffled. "I don't know."

"Let's ask Mama to call and order the right ones. The red ones." He smiled, like it was so easy. To him it was. To everyone else, it's always easy.

I nodded. "Okay." He held my hand as we walked downstairs to the living room.

Mama saw my long face and me holding Daddy's hand.

"Uh-oh. What's wrong?"

He explained about the glasses.

"Is that what took you so long? I'm surprised. I thought you would like the neutral color. Wouldn't draw as much attention."

I shook my head no.

"And you're sure about this? Really?"

I nodded yes.

"I see. Well, you don't have to be so shy, Jillian." She tickled my chin. "It's okay to say what you like, *in the moment.*" She stressed this last part, but I didn't respond.

"I wish this wasn't so hard for you," she said.

Me, too, I thought. Grammy said I'd grow out of my shyness, but since she left, it's only gotten worse. I'm supposed to grow out of it like a chicken grows out of goopy albumen and yolk. And then one day it breaks free. Right now it feels like I'll be a pool of goop forever.

Mama called and told Miss Boxy-Bushy we picked the wrong ones. She remembered us and changed the order right away.

"Well, that's that. They'll be ready in a couple of days," Mama announced.

My heart fluttered. I eked out a smile. One day next week

I will have glasses. Red ones. I will look confident and brave in my red glasses. Maybe I will feel it, too. And next week I might even tell Ms. W., yes, I'm a Mind Bender after all.

☆

Early on Sunday, Mama asked me again about weaving. "I'm sorry we skipped Keet's yesterday. You always get so many new ideas there. Why don't you try something small today? Get something on one of your empty looms."

"Maybe." I told her. *One day,* I thought.

It doesn't take long to weave something. The long part is deciding. Once I know I want to make something, I have to pick the colors. The patterns. Which loom to use.

This time I have to decide whether to weave or not. Technically, Mama is right. My looms are empty. But I can see a scarf right there on my favorite one. It's already made in my mind's eye. It's yellow and green and purple and blue.

It's confident and cheerful and bright.

It is the opposite of me.

When Grammy died, she had been sick a long time, slowing down, fading away. But as long as she could still sit up, she would weave. She had all kinds of looms—ones she made herself, ones she sat in her lap, big fancy ones.

She taught me how to weave as soon as I could hold yarn without eating it. Or as soon as I could sit still, I'm not sure which. She changed the story every time she told it.

Grammy gave me cardboard looms and lap looms to

61

practice on at first. Then we moved to more serious ones. When I got the hang of it, she gave me my own rigid heddle loom. Two of them! The smaller one is for bands and narrow strips. The larger one she called my "big girl" loom. It's my favorite. It sits on a special table in my room. I feel like a serious weaver when I use it.

The last thing I finished was a scarf for Grammy. Well, it was a little bigger than a scarf, but not as big as a wrap. Mama called it a shawl. It was ruby red, Grammy's color, with flecks of silver and white. I made it for her as a get-well-soon present when she came down with pneumonia. Something warm to cover her chest when she got a chill. I could tell she didn't feel good, but she smiled when I draped it around her. Two days later, she died.

They buried her with that scarf, that ruby red shawl. Daddy said she loved it as much as she loved me. How does he know? She died before she could say.

I haven't touched a loom since then.

I thought about weaving, and the Mind Bender, and being brave. I knew I would weave again eventually, but I didn't know what I would do about the Mind Bender. I was closer to a yes, but still not sure. I didn't really wanna ask my parents. They'd say *relax* and *you can do it.*

They don't get it.

Truth? Part of me wants to compete. Rashida isn't the only smart girl at Jemison. But the thought of proving myself makes my heart race. That part tells me not to bother. It's just a bunch of questions. Who cares?

Me, I guess. And Grammy. She would care.

I decided to ask Daddy what he thought. I wouldn't tell him the whole story. Just enough to get his ideas on what to do. I found him in the garage, cleaning his guitar. The bright stage lights framed him, like a solo act ready to perform to a huge crowd. His big, warm smile welcomed me.

"You coming to sing with me?"

"No."

"That's too bad."

I sat down on a stool across from him and studied the stage's wooden slats. He waited for me to say something, anything else. When I didn't, he asked, "What's on your mind?"

"I'm trying to pick between A or B at school."

"Do I get to know what A or B is?" He strummed the guitar strings softly.

"No."

He gave a hearty laugh. I guess it was a little funny, asking for help without explaining the problem. But I didn't want to tell him about Mind Bender yet.

"Okay, okay. How long have you been thinking about A or B?"

"A few days."

"Do you know what the answer is already?"

I looked at him. I wasn't expecting that question. But in a way I do know the answer. I'm just not *sure* sure.

"Well, kinda."

"Study long, study wrong!" He placed his guitar back on the stand.

"What does that mean?"

"It means being wishy-washy makes you weak. You waste the energy you could be using to act on your decision." He stood up now. "Make up your mind and go for it!"

"But what if I choose the wrong thing?"

"Does your heart know the right thing?"

My face tightened. "Maybe."

He nodded and smiled. Not like he was laughing at me, but like he understood something.

"Trust yourself, Jilly. If your heart knows what's right, you already have your answer. It's just up to you to commit to it." He kissed my forehead. "Buddha said, master your mind, don't let your mind master you."

CHAPTER TEN

Change of Heart

Mama loves everything about the moon. She says Mondays are moon days, and moon days are good days to try something new. I don't know why the moon equals new things, but she teaches this in one of her workshops.

Mama got really sick when I was little. She was diagnosed with something called lupus. When she felt better, she left her high-stress job and started her own business. Now people hire her to teach them all kinds of things related to leadership, self-care, and anything women want to know. I guess the moon fits in there somehow, too.

Today is Monday, or moon day. That means it's a good day to master my mind. It's a good day to be brave. To be confident in myself. To try, anyway.

Mondays mean low left ponytails and navy blue. I've never told this to my parents, but at Jemison, all the fifth grade girls look alike on purpose. We "twin." We wear the same hairstyles and the same kinds of outfits, like we're following a fashion calendar. Everyone blends in with everyone else. I don't know who started it. I just know that since sometime last year, everyone does it. I hate it.

One time Shelby didn't wear her hair the right way, and it was bad for her. I sat beside her at lunch, but she wouldn't speak or anything. She was too sad.

"Shelby thinks she's so cute today," girls whispered. She'd gotten her hair done for a wedding. It was still fancy, and there was no way her mom was letting her come to school in one of those plain-Jane styles. Later in the week, it was fine because by then, her flat twists and Shirley Temple curls were brushed back into a ponytail like everyone else.

So that's what I learned. Blend in. Go with the flow, or else. I wasn't surprised when they called me a crayon for wearing purple. But if colors are ever in style, they will tease you for wearing gray. They just make fun of anyone who is different. That's what I thought about Sunday night while Mama twisted my hair with shea butter and aloe vera.

I woke up Monday morning to super shiny twists. The sheen would give Rashida a run for her money, as Daddy would say. I stared in the mirror and willed myself to wear a twist-out like Mama does sometimes.

"Untwist it," I told the mirror. "You woke up early to do it." My hair would be big and wavy just like Miss Boxy-Bushy at the eye doctor. A shiny storm cloud instead of a calm ponytail to the left.

I put oil on my fingers, like Mama taught me, and unraveled the chunky twists one by one.

When I finished, I felt butterflies in my stomach, but I had a smile on my face. I hoped my parents wouldn't laugh. And worse, that Mama, the Decider, wouldn't decide it was too wild. If I could make it to the bus stop, it would be all good.

On my way to the kitchen I saw Mama's aqua blue wrap on the back of her office chair. I grabbed it and flung it around my shoulders like a cape. It was perfect. A cape to keep my courage up.

I stepped into the kitchen, where Mama and Daddy were already zooming around each other, fixing breakfasts and lunches.

They froze when they saw me. I froze back.

Daddy broke the ice. "Is today supermodel day at school?"

I smiled shyly. "Daddy!"

"I'm asking! You look great."

"And is that my wrap?" Mama wanted to know. "Is it cold in school?"

"No, I just . . . It's pretty."

"Of course it is. You made it! You go, girl." Mama said, giving me a high-five.

"You haven't worn your hair out in a long time. What's the occasion?" Daddy asked. "Is it picture day?"

"No. I just feel like being different."

"Is this about a boy?" Mama asked, getting serious and frowning.

"Yuck! Everyone knows boys are gross, Mama." *Marquez gets a pass because he's funny,* I thought.

"Just checking!" She laughed, throwing up both of her hands.

"You used to run around the yard with your hair out all the time," said Daddy. "Your mom could never comb it later. Is this the new thing at school?"

"No. You guys! I just don't want a ponytail today."

"Oh, I get it," said Mama. "It's Monday, right? Something new?"

"Yeah," I said, embarrassed now.

"Okay, okay. No more questions. I love it," said Daddy. "You should wear your hair like that whenever you feel like it."

"Thank you." I smiled. Bigger this time.

"Breakfast, then bus," said Mama, kissing my cheek.

"I know, I know."

CHAPTER ELEVEN
Pecking Order

I loved my bushy hair twisted out in wild waves. Even though part of me felt nervous, the rest of me felt powerful and strong and brave. Amazons must feel like this. I stood up tall, my imaginary dictionary steady on my head. The only thing missing were my Wonder Woman bracelets, to block the bad vibes. Just in case. Now, if I could only decide once and for all about Mind Bender . . . I owed Ms. W. an answer today.

In class, Ms. W. winked and gave me a thumbs-up.

Shelby stared, shocked at my new look, her eyes big and round. During morning work she whispered to me, "You wore your hair out?"

I nodded, remembering how sad she seemed last year when they teased her for her curls.

"I love it!" she said. "It's so . . . you!"

I patted my hair, grateful and embarrassed at the same time.

At recess I didn't play kickball or dodgeball or run any races. I felt like being upside down. I skipped over to the pull-up bars on the edge of the playground. Once in a while a few of us take turns flipping or hanging or doing pull-ups. Sometimes it's just me and Marquez. Today I was all alone, and that was fine by me. No blending in. No standing out. Just me, upside down. I could finally decide what to tell Ms. W.

I grabbed the metal bar in a chin-up, kicked both legs in front, and pulled over. *Like a junior Olympian on the uneven bars,* I thought, smiling to myself. I held on tight, pulling one leg at time across the bar, then eased back until I hung upside down by my knees. I watched the kickball game, minding my own business, swaying in the wind. I spied girls jumping rope near the basketball court. Then I spied a boy stomping in my direction.

I stopped swaying to watch him walk up from outta left field. I squinted until I could make out who it was. William.

He wormed up to the bar and then turned so he was looking out at the field. Never at me. "You know you can't win, right?" he said with a stank attitude.

Who does that?

I said nothing, so he repeated himself. Slowly, I guess in case I missed it.

"You. Can't. Win. I saw you practicing with the Mind Benders the other day. I heard you choked. Couldn't even answer the easy ones."

Anger radiated from my stomach. Sweat trickled down my back toward my neck.

"Everyone knows Rashida is the Mind Bender champion."

"Everyone?" I asked, giving him stank back. Even though I'd said the same thing to Ms. W., he had no right to say it to me. William is not the master of anything. He only came to be nasty, so he delivered his message and walked off.

"Everyone," he said, getting smaller by the second. "Even you. Especially you." He shouted that last part over his shoulder.

My head throbbed. I swung myself around and jumped off the bar. I landed on my feet, my mind made up. I would do the Mind Bender.

I heard someone gasp. "Whoa. Where did she learn to do that?"

Marquez jogged up to me. Recess was just about over and everyone had begun lining up.

"Hey." He nodded toward William, asking without words if I was okay.

I realized then that my fists were balled up, jaw locked shut.

"Hey," I managed back, saying without words, the worst was over. As we walked, I relaxed my fists, but not my jaw. I stopped and pointed in the air. "I don't know who William thinks he is, but he ain't my Mama."

Marquez nodded, agreeing.

"He don't tell me what 'everybody knows.'" Hands on my hips, big mad.

"What he think they know?" Marquez asked. Nosy classmates looked over.

I shrugged it off and lowered my voice. "Nothing."

He raised his eyebrows in a question, still wanting the answer.

"Nothing." I didn't tell him that I'd decided. "He don't know a single thing," I said.

"Zero things," said Marquez, slow and low. "Rien. Nada."

I giggled. "Zilch."

We high-fived on it, and he took off running, yelling over his shoulder, "Last one back is a rotten egg!"

"Boy, please!" I yelled as I sprinted to catch him, my hair bouncing behind me.

☆

"Today, inside the egg, the embryo is curled into a letter *C*. If all is going well, it starts to move. The bones are developing, and even the beak is beginning to form."

When Ms. W. said that, a few kids clucked. Then Marquez (who else?) and Shelby started pecking their heads out like chickens. Pretty soon we were all doing it. I think I even caught Ms. W. mid-peck, but then she adjusted her sparkly spectacles, so I wasn't sure.

"If everyone is on their best behavior, we will candle the eggs tomorrow," she said.

Candling is when you take a chicken egg, turn off all the lights, and, in a dark room, shine a light through the egg so you can see what's going on inside. Back in the day, the light would've been a candle.

"We don't use candles now. One, because that's fire and this is school," Ms. W. explained.

"And two, because that's a sure-fire way to bake a chicken. Get it?" said Jake, laughing.

"Or fry an egg," joked Marquez. People didn't know whether to laugh or be grossed out.

Shelby jumped up and folded her arms. "That's not funny!"

Rashida, of all people, told her to calm down, it was just a joke. William jumped in to agree, because of course he must agree with Her Majesty the Queen. I was just shocked Rashida said anything. She's always so serious. Defending jokes is not her style.

Ms. W. gave us all the death stare, and a hush fell over the room. "Thank you, Shelby. It's not nice to joke about everything." She glared at Jake and Marquez. "But you're right, real candles are dangerous. And they could harm the embryos."

We shifted in our seats, feeling bad about cooking the future chicks.

She went on to explain that even though it's basically a flashlight, you still call the process candling.

"Tomorrow we will see how many eggs are developing. And how many are not."

"What do you mean?" asked William.

Ms. W. peered at us over her glasses with that look my mom gives when she's tired of repeating herself.

"I've said all along, don't count your chickens, right? Well, until they are here and clucking around, you can't count them."

We hushed for real then.

"It's still too early to count them all in or out," she added, "but we'll get a look at what's going on inside." She threw me a Look, and I pretended not to notice.

After we all updated our journals, it was time to get ready to go home.

I slid over to Ms. W. while everyone packed their bags and shoved papers into their desks. I opened my mouth, but nothing came out. She kicked on the Wait Time and watched me, her eyebrows in the "invitation."

I thought about Grammy asking me to be confident in myself, Mama wanting me to speak up in the moment, Daddy telling me to master my mind. The only thing left for me to do was to open my mouth and tell Ms. W. what I decided.

I scanned the room to see if anyone was watching. There was William, pulling on his bookbag, relaxed and unbothered while I stood nervous and unsure. I took a deep breath.

"I'll do it," I said, firm but quiet, just above a whisper.

She smiled a tiny smile. "What was that?" she asked, though I knew she heard me.

"I'll do it," I said, a little louder this time.

"Mind Bender?"

"Yes, ma'am." I nodded and twirled a small lock of my wild hair.

She broke into a real smile and waved everyone on with the dismissal bell.

"That's my girl. Remember, just be yourself! Here are the rules." She handed one of the baby blue flyers. "And here's how you can see the Quizlets to review." She pointed to the QR codes at the bottom.

"It's all stuff you know. You just have to speak your mind, Jillian. Don't count yourself out."

Easier said than done. Twenty-two more days before May Day. Grammy's day. By then, I wanted to show Grammy I could believe in myself. I nodded, turned, and ran to the bus.

✰

I slid in beside Marquez. His regular seatmates were laughing and pointing at who knows what near the back. He was reading, but I knew he'd join in the fun as soon as the driver pulled away from school.

"Gonna do it," I whispered.

He looked at me for a second, his forehead wrinkled in confusion.

"Oh," he said, realizing. "Mind Bender?"

I nodded.

"That's what's up!"

"Yeah," I said. "You?"

"Maybe. Maybe not."

"Your big sister not trying to talk you into it?"

"She too busy trying to talk my mom into getting a cat."

"Your mom doesn't like cats?"

"She says it ain't a good time."

"My Mama likes 'em, but she's allergic."

"Daannng. We not getting a pet until we done with 'spring cleaning.' He rolled his eyes and made quotation marks in the air as he said it.

"How long will that take?"

He shrugged then, "Depends on my —"

Whack!

Someone smacked him in the back of the head. He turned around to start the usual afternoon foolishness.

I tuned them out, thinking. I wasn't sure if I should tell my parents about doing the Mind Bender. I wanted to keep it secret. If I choked, I choked, and that was that. On the other hand, they would know something was up and would ask me a million questions until they figured out what. If I did okay, they'd wanna know why I didn't tell them. I couldn't share updates, good or bad. I'd have to keep the whole thing quiet.

The more I thought about it, the more I knew it was better to just tell them. I brought it up while we were all in the kitchen before dinner.

"You guys promise not to overreact?" It was a question and an announcement all in one.

Daddy stopped chopping onions and Mama turned down the rice to simmer. They locked eyes, as if silently asking each other what I meant.

When neither one could explain anything to the other, they nodded at me, promising to remain calm and not get too excited.

"I had to decide between A or B."

Daddy's eyebrows went up, but he didn't say anything.

"A was compete in this year's Mind Bender. B was skip it."

Mama gripped her wooden spoon. I knew then that overreacting was still a possibility. But I rushed on.

"I picked A. I'm going to compete."

Mama caught herself mid-scream and turned it into a fake cough. Daddy kept it together with a quiet "That's my girl!" and a small fist pump.

"What's next?" he asked while Mama set the spoon down and smiled, looking calm, cool, and collected.

"I just have to study—quiz myself." I waved the now-wrinkled blue flyer around like it was no big deal.

"Are you nervous?" Daddy asked.

"Daddy—" I hid my eyes.

"What? Is that overreacting?"

"Yes. I don't wanna talk about it!"

"If you need help—" Mama started.

"If you want to practice—" said Daddy at the same time.

They looked at each other. I sighed.

"Proud of you, Jilly."

"Mama."

"I got it," she said. "No overreacting. Or no reacting at all, huh?"

Daddy snickered.

I frowned at him, and he threw his hands up.

"Okay, okay! Let's all underreact so we can get on with dinner, yes?"

"Yes!" Mama and I said together.

I pulled out dinner plates and began setting the table for three.

CHAPTER TWELVE
Heart of a Champion

Tuesday. Candling day. Time to take a real peek inside the eggs.

Ms. W. told us we had to wait until the end of the day, during our regular science period. She knew we were excited, but she said, "Time is precious. The embryos won't waste any of it. Neither should you."

They were growing hour by hour, and she wanted to give them a little more time before we took a look.

By recess, I was ready to be upside down again.

"You wanna hang with me today?" I asked Marquez, thumbing toward the horizontal bars. "Upside down?"

"Nah." He pointed to his book. "I'm almost done with this one. I'll read over there, though."

Marquez was reading another of his history books. He loves biographies of famous people. I can't believe he enjoys them so much. To me it's just a bunch of people and dates and things that happened a long time ago.

"Why do you like that stuff?" I asked.

His eyes got real big, and he scrunched up his face like he couldn't believe me. "Sérieux?"

"No French today, please." His mom's boyfriend is bilingual and has been teaching Marquez French. He springs it on us every chance he gets.

"Seriously? People can be amazing," he said. "Win against crazy odds. You know what that takes?"

I just looked at him.

"Heart," he said. "Not just any kinda heart. The heart of a champion." He pronounced *champion* with a French flair.

I rolled my eyes.

He pounded his chest. "Athletes are cool. King James. Usain. Pogba. Serena. But Ida B. Wells? Champion. She coulda died just for *writing* the truth."

"I've heard of her. Mama was glad when she won something called a Pulitzer Prize."

"Right! And Congressman John Lewis? Dude gave his whole heart."

"I definitely know about John Lewis. Plus I read *March*, and I don't even like comics."

Marquez shook his head. "Winning takes lot of work. That's why I love reading this stuff. Learning about it. You gotta train your heart to fight."

I pulled myself on the bar and flipped upside down.

"You ever give your whole heart to anything?" I asked him.

"Nah. Not yet." Joyful, smiling Marquez got serious. "I'm training, though," he said quietly.

"Your heart?" I asked.

He nodded, looking toward the school.

"Why?"

He sorta shrugged and then said, "The spring cleaning stuff."

"Why is that a battle?"

He shook his head. "Later."

"Promise?"

"Yeah."

I shot him a look. Unconvinced.

"I will! Anyway, *you* got one."

"Mind Bender," I agreed. "William says I got no chance of winning." My cheeks burned. I hated listening to William, but he was probably right.

"Who cares what he thinks? And anyway, you ain't got a chance of winning if you never say nothing."

"Ugh!"

"We all saw you choke. So how you gonna get ready for it?"

"Study, I guess."

"What's studying gon' do? You know all this stuff. You need to be training your heart to speak your mind."

He read a little bit while I swayed on the bar and thought about what he said. At last, I asked a question, sort of to him but sort of to myself, "What if that's not enough?"

He looked at me. "Nah. It's JTRA."

"What's that?"

"Something my moms says sometimes. JTRA—just the right amount."

I chewed on that and let myself daydream, swaying in the wind. I wondered if he was right. If being myself was really enough. Grammy thought so. That's what she wanted me to understand more than anything else. How could I train my heart to believe it?

☆

During science we discovered that the eye of the embryo should be visible now. We couldn't see the feet, but they have some, and today is the beginning of their toes. I never really thought about chicken toes, but I guess I do know what they look like.

Not only are their toes starting, but today the egg tooth begins, too. That's a little hard bump at the end of their beak. Chicks use it to break out of their shell when it's time to hatch. It falls off after they hatch and are out and about for little while. I sketched a picture for my science journal and thought about my response.

Chickens are born with all the tools they need to get free. We make fun of chickens, but I think chickens are wise. I wonder if people are as wise as chickens. I hope I have just the right amount of . . . courage? to get free.

After we finished our entries, Ms. W. put up bulletin board paper to cover the windows. She said we needed the room to be as dark as possible. While she did that, we washed our hands in the classroom sink, even though we weren't going to be touching the eggs today.

"Eggshells are porous," she said. "That means things like air and bacteria can get in. Including whatever is on our hands." We didn't want to do anything to endanger the embryos. Ms. W. washed her hands twice just in case.

We pulled our chairs into a big semicircle near the bright yellow incubator.

She stared us down through her golden glasses, daring anyone to move or breathe too hard. Then, one by one, she took out the eggs. She invited us in pairs to come and see them up close. She searched each egg for the air cell and blood vessels as signs of life.

Pair after pair went up, and everyone's eyes were big and smiley with lots of *ooooohs* and *ahhhs*.

Then Shelby and Marquez went up together. Ms. W. placed the egg on the candler and turned on the light. They froze. No oohing. No ahhing. No pointing. Even worse, Ms. W. froze, too, then leaned closer to inspect.

"It's empty?" Shelby whispered.

"I wouldn't say empty . . ." Ms. W. said slowly. "But you're right to be a little worried. I'm sorry to say, there doesn't seem to be much going on inside." Marquez and Shelby both looked dazed as they sat back down. Everyone did. But Ms. W. pressed on.

By the time she candled all twelve eggs, nine looked good. Three were "quiet," including mine and Scottie's. That's how she put it. Quiet.

"Does that mean they died?" Scottie asked what we all wondered.

"No," she said. "We can't count them out yet. And really, we can't say the others are good to go either. All we can do is send them love, and hope for the best."

✰

The bus drove away, leaving Marquez and me staring at each other. He hadn't gotten off at my bus stop in forever. He shrugged, smiling a little, flashing his dimple.

"I just felt like walking."

I nodded, and we started toward my house. It's a whole mile from my house to his, but he walks it sometimes to think about things. We matched each other step for step, not speaking at first. Finally I said something.

"Our chicks are quiet. I mean our eggs."

"Yeah. It's messed up."

"Is that why you're going the long way home?"

"Nah. I just don't feel like 'spring cleaning' yet." He did the air quotes again.

"What's the big deal?"

We walked a few steps, but he didn't answer. I looked over at him to see if he heard me. He didn't return the look, but he finally said something.

"We packing Dad's stuff."

"Whoa." I stopped walking. "I thought—didn't your parents split up a long time ago?"

Marquez stopped then, too, and turned around to face me.

"Yeah. He left a lot of stuff. Moms said he gotta come get it soon or we giving it all away. She said she gotta get on with her life." He turned around, and I rushed to get back in step with him.

"Dad said don't be giving all his stuff away. But when he comes to get us on weekends, he won't take one single box!" Each sentence was louder than the last.

"Sis is all upset. Moms is uptight. But we still packing."

I let that sink in awhile.

"I bet Mama will let me come help. Want me to ask?"

"Nah. Walking is good," he said, back at his normal volume.

"That's it?"

"Yeah. I got time to practice French. Think about cool cats like Kaep. Talk to my friends." He winked, then flipped it back on me. "That's what *you* gotta do to get ready for Mind Bender."

"Go walking? Learn French?" I giggled.

"Nah!" He laughed. You gotta do what *you* like! Doing stuff and thinking stuff that makes you feel good—that's heart training."

"Huh," I said.

We arrived at my yard then, Marquez smiling as we waved goodbye.

"See you tomorrow!" I called out from my door. "Let me know if you want help packing!"

"Au revoir!" he yelled back over his shoulder.

I waited, watching his backpack get a little farther away before I let myself inside.

CHAPTER THIRTEEN
New Sight

Not long after I finished my homework, the phone rang. Miss Boxy-Bushy called to say my glasses were ready. "That was quick," said Mama. We left to pick them up before the optometrist closed for the evening.

When we arrived, Miss Boxy-Bushy greeted us. The nickname still worked, but I wondered what her real name was.

"Welcome back!" she said, smiling and waving us in. "Red, right? Let's make sure they fit." She pointed to the glasses sitting in a little plastic tray, and then to the chair where she wanted me to sit.

She slid the red frames onto my face. Over and over she took them off, tugged, twisted, and adjusted the arms, and slid them back on. I kept feeling like I couldn't breathe. But I finally figured out that I was holding my breath. When she was satisfied they were centered and perfect in every way, she asked, "What do you think, Mom?"

Feeling a little dizzy, I turned my face to Mama. She was really, really clear now. I'd never noticed how fuzzy she was.

Mama nodded, her face breaking into a huge smile. She snapped her fingers. "I think those are sharp!" she said. "But you're the one wearing them. What do *you* think?" She motioned for me to look in the mirror and see for myself. Just then I saw Miss Boxy-Bushy's name tag. "Alicia Benjamin," I said out loud. I'd never noticed it before.

"That's me," she said, smiling, "the doctor's daughter."

I turned to the mirror and inspected my reflection. It was weird to see myself so clear and so close, but I have to admit, the glasses were cute! And red! And sassy!

Mama and Ms. Benjamin cooed when I smiled, which made me feel shy but happy at the same time. My cheeks burned.

Ms. Benjamin winked at me. "So did you get the right ones?"

"Yes, ma'am, but everything looks like I'm in a big bubble."

"Don't worry, that's normal. You'll get used to wearing them, and then you won't see the bubble anymore. But for now it might look like you're walking uphill everywhere."

Even with the bubble, I could see everything. I looked at myself in the mirror again and smiled. For real this time.

"You like them, Jilly Bean?"

I nodded.

"Good. I'll retwist your hair when we get home. New glasses, new hair."

We got an eyeglass case and some cleaning supplies and went back home.

☆

When we got home, I camped out in front of the nearest mirror, making duck lips and playing with my hair, until Daddy made fun of me.

"Who's hogging the mirror? Leave some for someone else," he teased. "Let me check you out, supermodel." He laughed, pretending to take pictures with an old-style camera.

"You like 'em?" I asked.

"The question is do *you* like them?"

"I think so—" I blushed, feeling shy again.

"What's wrong? They're great! You look stylish and smart. Don't you think so?"

"Yeah. But I wonder what other people will think." And just like that, I started to lose my nerve. William and the mean girls calling me four eyes while I try not to embarrass myself in the Mind Bender. *We all saw you choke.*

Dad noticed my slouching. He lifted my chin and squared my shoulders. "Hold on. Which people?"

"What?"

"You said 'I wonder what other people will think.' Which people? Because I already know what I think. And you're the only person who really matters. They're *your* glasses on *your* face."

I nodded, and dragged my feet upstairs to get my hair basket. Mama said she would do my hair and I could practice Mind Bender questions on her tablet.

Mama sat on the living room sofa, with me on the floor between her knees. She sprayed my hair with her homemade aloe vera conditioner and slowly combed it out section by section. After I swiped through a few sets of questions, she asked what was wrong. "Sit up straight. You're shrinking, Jillian. Why?"

"I don't know. I keep missing some of the hard ones," I admitted.

"That's okay, baby. You answer the ones you can, right? It's just the prelims."

"If you don't pass the prelims, you don't move up. I can't just get the easy ones right. That's not enough," I mumble.

"Enough for what? For who? If you tell me this is about Rashida or other people . . ."

"Mama."

"Jillian." She was getting annoyed.

"Yes, ma'am?"

She finished another twist before she said another word.

"You should really weave something. Something small. Anything."

"Why?"

"Because you loved it."

"You don't weave," I said.

"No, but I write and teach instead. Your father plays music. We all have *something*. Weaving is *your* something. It's how you express yourself."

I didn't know what to say, so I sat there. She started the next twist.

"When you have a *something* and you do it, it teaches you to know yourself better."

"But I know how to weave."

"Yes, but you don't know *yourself*. I'm watching you get quieter and smaller, week after week. You were proud of yourself when you weaved. More confident."

I didn't really get what she was saying, but I nodded anyway. I practiced a few more questions while she finished twisting my hair. I only missed a few, but each one seemed to warn me that Mind Bender was a bad idea. I was starting to think I had made a mistake telling Ms. W. yes.

When I got ready for bed, I looked over at my loom. Something red caught my eye. I plucked it from a basket and felt sad as soon as I recognized it. When I made Grammy's scarf, there were scraps left over. I used a lap loom to weave them into this headband or small belt—I'm not sure what it is. Grammy died, and I forgot all about it. I inspected it, then tossed it on my nightstand.

I looked in the mirror. At my frowny face. At the red

glasses that didn't match anything. *What's wrong with blending in?* I asked myself. *Wearing beige and ponytails. Everyone does it. Even Rashida.*

Marquez said I should be myself. Myself is a shy girl who doesn't like attention. These glasses will draw attention. The Mind Bender will draw attention. I'll be a bright red, four-eyed choking chicken.

I'm sorry, Grammy, I thought. *Red is your color, not mine. And Mind Bender is Rashida's thing, not mine.* I made it this long without red glasses and without beating Rashida at anything. Maybe I can stick to weaving and tell Ms. W. never mind when I get to school in the morning.

I placed the glasses gently on my nightstand, turned off my light, and tried to sleep.

CHAPTER FOURTEEN

JTRA

I woke up with a stomachache and a pounding heart. I wasn't really ready to give up on my promise to Grammy to be more confident in myself, and to not worry so much about what other people think. It was the first official day of Mind Bender—the preliminary round. After prelims, the top two from every class go to Round 1. By the end of all the rounds, there are two winners for the whole school—one for the Little Leagues (K through second grade) and one for the Big Leagues (third through fifth grades). The Big League winner is officially the Mind Bender champion.

I sat up in bed, deciding what to do next. I hated the in-between feeling. I wanted to be brave, but I didn't want to mess up. I wanted to blend in, but I wanted to wear my pretty red glasses after all. I wanted to wear my hair the way I wanted to wear my hair. I just wanted to be Jillian.

Be Jillian. The more I thought about it, the more I knew that's what I had to do. Grammy said it. Ms. W. said it. Marquez tried to tell me, too. Daddy. Mama says I'm her smart, beautiful daughter. I just wish she could add brave, too.

I remembered William's nonsense on the playground. I started to get angry again. *Everyone knows . . .* No, they don't. I'm just as smart as Rashida is. I know what she knows. I can do what she does. I know Mama said it's not about what's "out there." But in here, I knew my stomach hurt and if I didn't get up soon, Mama would ask me questions and I would miss my bus. I sighed. *There's twenty days 'til May Day —Grammy's memorial day,* I told myself. *No more hiding.*

I rushed to get dressed. I put on a white MOTIVATE THE PLANET T-shirt and my red glasses. I looked in the mirror and smiled. I couldn't help it. They were pretty funky, I had to admit. The hairstyle of the day was the single high ponytail. *At least for everyone else.* Feeling a little bolder, I quickly loosened the twists from overnight and picked through my hair. Then I saw it. The red scrap sitting on my nightstand. *It would be cute as a headband,* I thought. It was just the right length —JTRA, as Marquez would say. I tied it around my head. It felt just right. Seeing myself, feeling myself pulled together, calmed me down. A little, anyway. My heart slowed and my stomach eased up.

On my way out the door, my parents wished me luck on the prelims. Daddy high-fived me and called me a supermodel genius. Mama kissed me and reminded me to take deep breaths when I got nervous. Today's bravery outfit:

bright red glasses and big hair, with a bright red band from Grammy's scarf. Mind Bender, here I come.

✮

"Look at Jillian, she's wearing glasses!"

Shelby didn't sound mean when she made the grand announcement, but I cringed anyway. Rashida smiled, but I have to admit, she didn't look like she was laughing at me. More like she thought the glasses were cool.

I unpacked my bookbag, sorta smiling and sorta hiding at the same time.

William, whose mama never taught him to say nice things or be quiet, called out, "Oh look, another pair of eyes. Now you're just a four-eyed—"

"Yo man, relax," Marquez interrupted.

"Oh, is that your girlfriend now?" said William, his cheeks flushing red.

"Nah. But she is my friend."

I smiled. Marquez is cool.

Jake jumped in, "William just mad because he don't have one."

"Ohhhh!" Now everyone was in on it.

"Settle down, class," called Ms. W. She does not deal with foolishness for very long. "Pretty glasses, Jillian." She smiled, touching her slick frames in a salute. How could I forget that she wore glasses, too?

"Thank you." I stood a little taller then. Just a smidge.

95

When I sat down beside Marquez, he was all smiles. "You look ready!" he said.

"What does that mean?"

"You look . . . like you! Everyone tryna be like everyone else. But you look like Jillian. It's dope."

"Thanks! But . . . what's wrong with fitting in?" I asked.

"Nothing. But you can just be you. And wear wavy hair on ponytail day."

I blinked. "Wait! How do you know about that?" I giggled.

"I have a sister? Look. It's twin day every day. Like we got school uniforms or something. It's weird."

"The boys don't do it, though."

"Nah, but no one really got their own style."

"My mama would say kids don't *really* have style anyway."

"I dunno." He shrugged. "But you gotta be yourself. Not do what everybody else is doing. Like Colin Kaepernick." He pointed to Colin's biography lying on his desk. "Dude is true to himself."

I rolled my eyes at him. "You think you so smart."

"Duh! Readers make leaders!"

"Less talking, more working, you two," Ms. W. scolded us from across the room.

"I read books, too," I whispered out the side of my mouth.

"Yeah, but . . ." Marquez whispered back, "history and biography. That's where it's at."

"Gross."

"One day you'll thank me," he said, brushing his shoulders. "You're welcome!"

I rolled my eyes again and looked at the board. It was super easy to see today's morning work.

☆

The morning flew by. And before long, it was time. Prelims weren't during recess or off to the side. They were in class. In front of everyone.

We set up chairs across the front, like a real competition. There were seven of us—Rashida, Shelby and Jake, Scottie, Allan, Hank, and me. Marquez, who did the practice round for fun, said he had enough fun already, so he'd just watch.

I tried not to panic, hoping my heart wouldn't break free from my body 'cause it was beating so fast. I twirled a lock of hair, but it didn't help. I still felt nervous and fidgety.

We began with a warm-up round. I'm sad to say, I wasn't very warm. Cold. Frozen, really. I couldn't move or say anything. I felt and saw everyone staring at me. But nobody more than Ms. W.

I ran out of time and didn't give an answer to my warm-up question. The way she drilled her eyes into my soul, I felt she was candling me with her golden glasses to see the goopy egg yolk inside my shell. *Are you growing or not?* she seemed to shout. *Is there life in there?*

I didn't know.

We started the free-for-all. Rashida was the first to score.

97

She shouted her answer in a strong, clear voice. The same voice that yelled out "DONE!" And "Yum! The sweet taste of victory!" Every syllable loud and proud.

I scowled, jealous that she could just speak her mind that way. No wasting time prying it out. *Wham* in her brain. *Bam* out her mouth. For me there's a jumble of too-big words, then a fight to get them out of my head and into the world. I frowned even more.

But just then Marquez caught my eye and pretended to sneeze. Except he said "JTRA" instead of "achoo." Everyone else said "bless you," but I heard him. I laughed. Still nervous, but it helped. A lot.

JTRA. Just the right amount. I pushed my glasses higher on my nose and sat up straighter. *Train your heart. Speak your mind.* I nodded to myself. We continued. This time, I fought.

We battled question by question. Many times Rashida won. Sometimes one of the others. But pretty often? Me. It was a competition, fair and square. In the end, Rashida took first place.

Guess who took second?

When Ms. W. announced the end of prelims, everyone clapped. The competitors clapped. Ms. W. clapped. Marquez gave me a thumbs-up. And me and Rashida, my sworn enemy, my foe, we looked at each other and smiled.

CHAPTER FIFTEEN

Fly Away

"You always hang on those bars or race or play kickball. Why don't you jump rope?"

I couldn't believe it. Rashida and I were talking! Actually talking to each other during recess!

I thought about how to explain. "Have you ever dreamed of flying?" I asked. "Not in an airplane—you, like Superman, just flying."

Rashida shook her head but smiled. Not like she was laughing at me, but like it might be really cool to fly.

"When I'm running fast or hanging upside down or swinging high, I feel like I'm with the wind. It's the closest I can get to flying. I love it."

Rashida nodded. Her forehead wrinkled, as if she were trying to imagine it for herself.

"What does jump rope feel like?" I asked. "I mean, I've done it, but what does it feel like to you?"

"Not like flying, but it's fun. Come jump." She lowered her voice to a whisper and leaned in. "I'll show you a surprise."

I stared at her, my mouth open. She winked. I laughed and followed her.

Janice and Shelby turned the long rope as one girl after another jumped in. Every jumper sang her own jump rope song, and the rest of us were backup singers. Even I knew all the words and joined in. When Rashida's turn came, she jumped in, singing my favorite, "Miss Mary Mack." And then she danced, with big jumps and little jumps and a whole routine! She really danced. Janice and Shelby laughed and kept up with her, turning without missing a beat. The rope disappeared with her moves. The other jumpers laughed and cheered, and even some of the dodgeball kids stopped to see what the fuss was about.

When she finished, she ducked out of the rope and struck a pose. Wakanda Forever! I almost fell out. Perfect Rashida, being completely silly. And who knew she had moves? I tried to high-five her, but she waved instead. She smiled so big, I knew it wasn't a diss. She just didn't know any better.

"Where'd you learn to do that?" I asked.

"Valerie and I make up jump dances at home," she said, catching her breath. "But our mother says we have to have the right decorum at school."

"Decorum?"

"That means don't do anything to embarrass her."

"But that was great! I'll never look at jump rope the same way again."

Rashida threw her head back and laughed. It was a deep belly laugh, not the way she usually covers her mouth and giggles in class. Not prim and proper. No decorum. Just joy.

So Rashida is not at all like I imagined. She jumps and dances and laughs. I am not ready to call her my *friend*, but maybe she is not my *foe* either.

☆

I ran home from the bus, still happy about my "win." I smiled as I rushed past the blur of pink azaleas blooming. They looked even prettier than usual today.

When I finally burst into the house, I found Mama putting sliced apples and peanut butter on a plate and singing to herself.

"Look at you." She smiled. "My little sunbeam! So how did the prelims go?"

"Well, I was scared at first and worried about looking stupid. But I dunno. My friend, Marquez, made me laugh, so I relaxed a little."

"That's so nice of him." She smiled and nodded, encouraging me to continue.

"I didn't know the answer to every question, but I did know a lot of them. We had warm-ups where the teacher would call your name and give you your own question. And then we had the Fair and Square round. Whoever answered, got it. I froze at first. Anyway, Marquez did this funny thing and I shook it off. And now I'm going to Round 1!"

"Yay! I knew you could do it. Congratulations!" Mama tickled my chin. "And the glasses were okay?"

"Yeah!" I yawned, suddenly feeling tired. "A few people noticed, but it was okay."

"Good! Well, Jilly Bean, I have a little more work before I call it a day. Are you yawning?"

"Just a little." I yawned again, and we both turned when we heard music coming from the garage. "Is that Daddy?"

"Yeah, go say hi. He finished a huge project so he got off early today. He's just banging around."

I skipped to the garage just as he started strumming the opening chords to "Fly Away," another favorite from Lenny Kravitz. It was the perfect song for how I felt right then.

I walked out dancing, snapping my fingers to the beat. Daddy laughed and nodded, then started to sing. I joined in, singing about flying above trees and anywhere I please.

We sang loud and proud and full of joy.

At the end, we punched the sky like we were in a real rock concert. I was sweating and laughing and glad for that red headband keeping my hair back.

"There's my Jilly Bean! Good day?"

"Yep! I made it to the next round of Mind Bender!"

"There's my girl!" We high-fived. "Can't wait to hear more about it. You staying for another song?"

"Nah." I cleared my throat. "Maybe later. I just wanted to say hi!"

"Love you!" He blew a kiss.

I left as he began another song.

Up in my room, I pulled off the red headband and twirled it around. I thought about the scarf. The one I "saw" on my empty loom the other day. I pulled out a basket of yarn and picked out two pretty bundles from my stash. One was a sparkly mix of aqua, green, and purple. The other was a shimmery canary yellow.

You never know how it's gonna turn out when you mix yarns. It's an adventure. I like to be certain about everything else. I like to know for sure. That's one reason I get so nervous. I don't like it when I don't know how things'll turn out.

But weaving is different. When I weave, I take chances. It feels like flying. It's weird, but I lose time thinking, creating, imagining things in my mind. I am floating above everything. I am free.

CHAPTER SIXTEEN
Walking on Eggshells

The last thing I remember was daydreaming about weaving, so I was confused when my alarm went off in the morning. I guess Mama tucked me in.

Even though I slept all that time, I kept yawning. I felt trapped in molasses, but I did my best to hurry up and get dressed. Mama kept calling me a slowpoke, so I guess it wasn't working.

When I got to school, everyone seemed nicer than usual. They smiled and nodded at me. Then I realized I wasn't looking at the floor so much. Maybe they are always that way. Maybe I never look up.

We started the day with math, as usual, but then we spent the rest of the morning starting language arts and social studies projects: civil rights magazines. We had to write and draw about people, artifacts, and events from that era.

It was fun, except that Marquez thinks he knows everything about it. He tried to tell Shelby what to do, and let's just say she didn't wanna hear it. She yelled at him to leave her alone. He laughed it off, like no big deal, but his eyes weren't smiling.

"What's wrong?" I whispered. He shrugged and went back to work on his own magazine. No one said much after that.

Finally it was egg time. Ms. W. announced that we would candle again tomorrow and see if some of the quiet ones can be counted in. If the air cells are growing, she will mark them, and we will assume they are still potential chicks. Ms. W. projected a picture of the embryo at day nine, and we pulled out our journals to take notes.

The eggs are getting more porous every day. This makes it easier for oxygen and germs to get inside. The embryos are getting stronger, but the eggshell is more fragile. So we have to be extra careful.

Ms. W. said that people are the same way. "When we are more open, we can have new experiences and see things differently. That can help us grow and make us stronger, too."

But when you're open, you're more fragile. It's easier for you to get hurt. She didn't say that last part, but I know it's true. That's what happened when Grammy died. Especially after I gave her the scarf. Letting her love flow to me and my love flow to her, I was open. Fragile.

Now I'm feeling open again, when maybe the shell is the right thing. Should I be fragile with Rashida? My foe, my sworn enemy. She smiled at me yesterday and gave me a hopeful look. Not like she hoped she would win, but like she hoped—we could be friends. But Rashida has a sister and William and people following her every move. Why would she need or want other friends?

I swallowed, but it felt funny. Scratchy.

☆

I yawned during dinner.

"You're still sleepy?" Mama asked. "Are you getting up in the middle of the night?"

"No, ma'am," I said. The three of us sat at the kitchen table. My eyes were on my plate, but I felt Mama and Daddy's eyes on me.

"You feel okay?" Mama reached up and touched my forehead, frowning.

"I'm just tired."

"You're not eating either," Daddy pointed out.

I always love his cooking, and today it was Cajun shrimp, which is yummy. But I couldn't swallow.

"I'm trying."

"Your food is skating around your plate, but it's not going inside you," he said.

"You don't have a fever," said Mama, "but this is two days now. I wonder if you're getting sick."

I shrugged. I just wanted to go to sleep. I never get sick, except that one time I had chickenpox in second grade.

"Maybe it's nerves. Are you stressed out?" she asked.

Mama's really big on stress. It can make her lupus flare, and she could get really sick. Like hospital sick. But she says stress isn't good for anyone. Even young people have to watch out.

I am nervous, but I don't say so. Tomorrow is Round 1 for the Mind Bender. The top ten winners from each grade level compete.

"I'm just tired," I said again. I wanted this thing to hurry up and be done. Being brave takes a lot of work.

I pretended not to see them eyeing each other across the table. Speaking in that secret parent language. Worrying eyes now. Worrying whispers later, when I'm not here. I ate another bite of shrimp and a tiny bit of broccoli.

And was it my imagination or did Mama look a little rundown, too? She's always a bright light, but tonight she seemed dimmer somehow.

I finally gave up on dinner and asked to go to my room.

I looked in the mirror. I have to admit, I looked as sleepy as I felt. I was too tired to think about a bravery outfit or a hairstyle for tomorrow, or about practicing any questions.

I grabbed the bundles of yarn I picked out yesterday and tossed one and then the other in a sleepy juggle. Up and down, up and down. They were little roller coasters, like my stomach feels when I am nervous. They were flying, just like I do when I am happy.

I hugged them and curled up again, dreaming of Lenny songs and yarn and chickens and eggs.

CHAPTER SEVENTEEN
Speaking Up

I didn't hear my alarm.

Oh no! I jumped out of bed, shocked at the sunlight brightening my room. *Shouldn't it still be dark?* I tripped on a basket of yarn and tumbled to the floor, landing in a pile of bundles.

Mama heard the noise and rushed in to make sure I was okay. I wasn't. Then she made it worse. "You were so pitiful last night, and then you slept through your alarm."

I sat on the floor, my eyes opening wider the more she talked.

"I let you sleep," she said. "You just need to stay home today. Rest would do us both some good."

I opened my mouth to complain, and guess what? Nothing came out. Not even a peep! I tried again, and out came this weird squeak thing. I tried to say no, but it sounded more like a rusty door swinging open in the dead of night. Or a tiny puppy in a bad mood.

"My goodness. You lost your voice? You're definitely home for the day."

I shook my head no, pulled myself up, and put my glasses on. Dug into my bookbag and snatched out a sheet of paper and pen. Mama watched as I scratched a note in big letters:

MIND BENDER IS TODAY!
I HAVE TO GO TO SCHOOL!

"No honey, you can do it tomorrow."

I underlined <u>HAVE TO</u> and held up the sign again. Pointing this time.

"Stop yelling at me, Jillian," she said, even though I was only writing. I huffed, and she didn't like that either.

"Relax," she said. "Go back to sleep. There's nothing that won't wait until tomorrow."

I squinted at the sign, confused. Maybe I left out a word. Maybe it wasn't right. But no, all the words were there. I held it up once more, demanding she read it again. Mama shook her head no and left me standing there. The Decider had decided. I plopped on my bed and cried silent tears.

I couldn't believe it. A million thoughts flooded my mind.

What if I don't go to school?

What if I let down Ms. W.? Or Marquez?

What if I miss the candling of the chicks?

What if I don't have to say anything or speak my mind?

What if I just skip today, this week, and the rest of this year and pretend Mind Bender never happened? Can I just sleep and weave and sing songs with Daddy?

Maybe I'm sick because I don't really want to do this speaking up, being myself thing. Maybe I like it better in my shell.

I stood up and frowned in the mirror. Even my cheerful red glasses didn't cheer me up. I felt confused. Glad and sad to be home. Like the Last Person Standing, I felt like I won/lost. *You promised, Jilly. Promised Grammy you'd really try.* What would Marquez say? What would his champions do?

Train your heart.

I looked around my room for ideas. Something that would make my heart feel strong. I saw the red headband. My favorite loom. *I do miss weaving. I have to start again, soon.*

I pictured myself weaving, running, flying. Doing things I loved. I felt warmer. Happy. I could actually feel the smile on my face.

I tried the opposite just to see what would happen. I pictured myself being shy, thinking things but not saying them. Letting other people win. I didn't like that feeling—the feeling of a sinking stomach. *Your stomach always knows the truth.* I heard Mama's voice in my mind.

I sat back down and turned my note over.

DEAR MAMA,
I DON'T WANT TO STAY HOME TODAY.

I WANT TO DO THE MIND BENDER INSTEAD.
I AM VERY NERVOUS ABOUT IT. EVEN
THOUGH I FEEL SCARED, I WANT TO WIN
— OR AT LEAST TRY. PLEASE LET ME GO
TO SCHOOL. IF MY VOICE IS BACK BY
LUNCH, CAN I GO?
   LOVE, JILLY

I read it twice to make sure it was poised, with no shouting. I walked the note to her office. Handing it to her, I stood still while blood beat in my ears. In my chest. I wanted her to say yes, I could go, but part of me still wanted her to say no, I couldn't. Then I'd be off the hook.

She read my note and sighed. Touched my forehead. Lifted my chin so my eyes met hers.

"Well, you still don't have a fever," she said, rubbing her forehead. "I don't know how you can do it if you can't actually talk. Isn't this a verbal game?"

I nodded.

"Are you sure you want to do this?" she asked.

I looked at the floor and shook my head no. *I'm not.*

"But you want me to take you to school anyway?"

I looked inside my mind to be sure. *What other chances would I have? May Day is coming whether I give up now or not.* I nodded my head yes.

"Hmmm." She took her time in answering, but she finally said something.

"I don't know what will happen, but yes, if you're feeling up to it, I'll take you to school around lunchtime. Proud of you, kiddo."

Together we googled sore throats and laryngitis. I gargled with warm salt water and drank hot tea with honey. I needed to be very quiet and rest my voice. Sleep is quiet. I took a nap.

☆

When I woke up, I sounded like a whispering frog, but at least something was coming out. I wouldn't have to say much during the competition, only when called. I wouldn't have to talk over anyone. And worst case, I could write my answers. I had it all figured out.

Mama took me to school as promised. She signed me in and kissed me for courage. I couldn't help thinking she still didn't look quite like herself, but I didn't say anything about it. I just kissed her back.

When I got to class, they were coming back in from recess. Marquez and Jake and even William made weird faces I couldn't read. Shelby shouted out, "There she is!"

"Surprised to see you around here," William mumbled. He looked me up and down, as if he'd found me in the wrong part of town after dark. Marquez just raised his eyebrows and jutted his chin as a hello. "Hey," I croaked back at him. He covered his mouth in shock.

I pointed at my throat, and Shelby, always loud, said, "You lost your voice!" It wasn't a question. She proclaimed it as if it were an important announcement to a crowd. The whole class looked at me, and then everyone began buzzing like bees. My heart thumped, my stomach lurched, and Ms. W. appeared from nowhere, grabbing my shoulders.

"Start back on your magazine projects," she told everyone else.

"Your voice—is that why you're late?" she said only to me. Her eyes looked big and round behind her glasses, and I felt her tight grip on my shoulders, but her voice remained calm and even.

I nodded.

She nodded back and pulled off my bookbag while pushing me to the door.

"Well, the good news is, you made it in time. If you still want to compete, the next round begins in five minutes."

I didn't have time to panic, but I did anyway. I spun to face her and spun away. Then back to her again. *Running around like a chicken with . . .* I couldn't even let myself finish the thought.

I stared at her, frozen. *May Day*, I thought. Then I remembered the universal distress call. If I said *mayday* three times fast, would I disappear? Would Grammy send me a sign to say I'd done enough?

"Library—go!" said Ms. W., giving me a gentle push. "Rashida's already there."

"The champion waits for no one." William called out, his arms folded, watching the scene.

"Man, be quiet sometimes!" said Marquez.

"Wait!" yelled Shelby. "You need—something. She can't talk. Shouldn't she take a mini board?" She meant the little white dry-erase boards we used sometimes in class.

"Good thinking," said Ms. W.

Marquez ran to the counter and grabbed one, plus two dry-erase markers. He jogged back over and pushed them at me.

"Go get 'em, champ. And shake a tail feather! Whatever you do, don't chicken out!" He laughed at his corny jokes, and I have to admit, they made me giggle. A little. Ms. W. grabbed my shoulders again, spun me around, and pushed me into the hallway.

Mayday, mayday, mayday. I took off, running for the library.

CHAPTER EIGHTEEN

Keep Hope Alive

The other nine players sat in gleaming wooden chairs arranged in front of the Milky Way mural. Three long tables stretched end to end in front of the chairs. Rashida sat on one end. A boy I didn't recognize sat on the other. I took the one empty chair near the middle. Scratch paper, pencils, and a buzzer lay in front of each person. I added my whiteboard and markers to my pile.

I had no idea how this would work out.

"We thought you were absent," said Mr. Kline, the librarian.

I shook my head.

"You're from Ms. Warren's class, right?" asked Mrs. Daniel. She's Jemison's math coach and the official Mind Bender scorekeeper.

I nodded.

I couldn't tell for sure, but I felt Rashida leaning forward to look at me. Probably everyone was. My glasses blocked my side view. The optometrist warned that my peripheral vision wouldn't be so good now.

I kept my eyes on Mr. Kline.

"Cat got your tongue?" he asked.

"Sort of," I whisper-croaked, and pointed to the board. For sure I heard giggles on both sides as everyone figured out my problem.

The librarian's eyes got big, and he opened his mouth to speak. I guess he changed his mind because he nodded and began. He quickly read the rules. There would be fifty questions, some representing every subject. He wasted no time getting to question number one.

"Name the three states of matter."

There are more than three, but I knew the answer he meant—solid, liquid, and gas. I uncapped my marker and scribbled, but three other kids beat me to the buzzer. Rashida gave the correct answer before I could finish writing mine down.

On the next question—give two examples each of conductors and insulators—I hit the buzzer as soon as I could. I figured if he called on me, I'd have time to write my answer. I was wrong. Mr. Kline did call on me, but I didn't finish "stating" my answer within ten seconds. So even though I'd already written silver and copper for conductors, he called on someone else.

I started to panic. Writing wouldn't work. I was gonna

need a better strategy, and quick. I'd have to use my voice or just sit here and lose. On the next question I told my heart to slow down and got ready to push out the answer. My shaky hand hovered over the buzzer.

But it didn't matter.

Charlayne Hunter-Gault and Hamilton Holmes were the first two Black students to attend the University of Georgia. It took me only a second to remember, but that was a second too long. Jitters and frozen thoughts waste time. I felt defeated. Like I could've stayed in bed after all.

But then something happened. The kid who got it right danced! He hit a quick *Whoa* right there in his chair. We all busted out laughing. Even him. Even me. And then I felt a little better.

I told the mean judge inside to leave me alone so I could think in peace.

As it turned out, Mr. Kline tossed out a math question next. And a word problem at that! Everyone began scratching on paper, with me gliding on the whiteboard. I hit the buzzer first and punched my board straight up. Mr. Kline nodded as he awarded me the point. *Yes!*

From then on, I decided I either I knew the answer or I didn't, so no more hesitating. *Spit it out or sit it out,* I told myself. Except for math, I whisper-croaked my answers when I had the chance. I was first to name two figures from the Harlem Renaissance, author Zora Neale Hurston and Mr.

Everything Paul Robeson. He was good at school and was an athlete, entertainer, and activist.

There were plenty of questions I didn't answer because I was too slow or didn't know. But I did my best. Grammy would be proud.

Before long, Mr. Kline announced the end.

"Great job, everyone," he said. We sat there on those hard wooden chairs and waited. Mrs. Daniel tallied scores by hand, and Mr. Kline used a scorekeeping app. Then they switched and checked each other's work. Everyone else chatted and joked while I sat still, fighting the urge to disappear.

"Ten of you participated today," said Mrs. Daniel. Everyone hushed up in a hurry. "As you know, the top five will go on to Round 2."

I felt lightheaded. I really wanted to get to the next round. For Grammy. For me, too.

Mr. Kline stood up to make the announcement. "Congratulations to Jared, with 70 points. Kyle, also 70 points. Ryan, 80 points. Jillian, 120 points. And last but not least, Rashida, our top scorer, with 160 points!"

Mrs. Daniel said something after that, but I didn't hear it. The *Whoa* dancer made it. Rashida made it, of course, and I made it, too!

Everyone got certificates for finishing the round, and those were also our hall passes. Rashida shook everyone's hand. Even mine. Then we walked back to class together.

"I can't believe you lost your voice," she said, her eyes wide in disbelief.

"Me neither," I whisper-croaked.

"You kept up pretty well. For a quiet girl," she joked.

I smiled at her double meaning.

"Why are you so quiet, anyway?" she asked. "I don't just mean today."

I shrugged. "Feels like being onstage," I whispered. "Everyone's watching, and what if I say something dumb?"

"Have you ever been onstage?"

Singing in the garage didn't count. I shook my head no, feeling embarrassed because she would probably say I didn't know what I was talking about.

"My aunt is a professional speaker. She says if you get stage fright, you have to think of something funny."

I thought about that. I did calm down when that boy danced in his chair.

"Make yourself laugh." She sounded so sure of herself, but her eyes were smiling. "It relaxes you."

"Yeah, I'm starting to notice that. But what if nothing's funny?" I croaked.

"I guess you could think about it ahead of time. Pull it out when you're ready."

I nodded. We walked in silence.

"Thanks," I whispered, really meaning it. I even made eye contact.

"No problem. Congrats, by the way."

"You, too!" I croaked, pointing at her, even though my other fingers were pointing back at me. But she got the message.

"Remember to figure out something funny. *Two* funny things. Don't put all your eggs in one basket." She winked. Jump rope dancing and bad jokes? I definitely didn't know Rashida was like this.

We went into the classroom, laughing. Or in my case, with no voice, smiling as big as I could.

☆

Just like last time, Ms. W. taped bulletin board paper over the windows to darken the room like last time.

One by one she candled the chicks. Her main goal was to check on the ones that weren't really growing earlier this week, but she checked them all just to be sure.

We went in pairs again. Everyone wanted to see the same eggs they saw before. We actually took turns holding the eggs this time. They were warm from the incubator. Then Ms. W. placed each egg on the candler so we could see inside.

Here's what they look like when you candle them:

We started off with twelve eggs. The first time we candled, nine were growing. Three were not. We heard the other teachers had two or three blanks last time, too.

This time, one of our blanks—Marquez and Shelby's—had vessels and stuff inside! Better late than never. We added one more potential to the group, so now we're up to ten. The other two, including mine, still looked empty. Ms. W. said we shouldn't stop hoping for them yet.

I wonder if they are shy and do not like all this attention. Maybe they have a better chance of growing if they can relax. Ms. W. said hope and patience are all we have right now.

I guess we'll see.

CHAPTER NINETEEN
Perchance to Weave

"How'd it go today, Jilly Bean?" Daddy woke me from a nap, offering a mug of hot tea. I gave him a thumbs-up.

"Is your voice still gone?"

I nodded, rubbing my eyes and sitting up. "I whispered. But guess what?" I croaked. "The top five from the grade go to the next round. I made it!"

"That's my girl!" We high-fived.

"I had to beg Mama to let me go," I croaked.

"Good," he said. He didn't blink or laugh or anything. Just kept smiling like that was normal.

"Why?" I whined. "I was scared. I almost missed it."

"Good."

I just looked at him then. Good? I knew the word, but it didn't make sense.

"You're looking at this the wrong way," he said. "Grammy always said what? Have an attitude—"

"Of gratitude," I mustered.

"Gratitude, right." He sat down beside me. "First, Mama loves you with her whole heart. She doesn't want you sick and stressed out. She'll be worried and stressed out, too, which is not good for her lupus. And then who else will be worried and stressed?" He pointed to himself. "This guy."

I nodded yes.

"She wanted to protect you, to let you rest. She did what she thought was best. But it was important to you. So when she said no, what did you do?"

"I begged her to let me go."

"You had to fight for yourself. You had to speak up."

I nodded again, but I still didn't see his point.

He looked at me with one of his sideways smiles. The kind he gives when he's waiting for you to get the joke. "How did it turn out?"

"Fine."

"No monster came and gobbled you up?"

"Daddy."

"She took you! You made it in time — and you won! Right?" He laughed.

"Yeah," I whisper-laughed back.

"Yeah! I think you should tell Mama thank you. For taking good care of you and helping you speak up for yourself. Okay?"

"I guess."

"Dinner's ready. Let's go eat."

★

Trance: When you're aware of things, but you're sorta not. When you tune in to one channel on the radio and you can't hear anything else. Not your mama calling you, not your daddy playing his guitar. When you're so into what you're watching on TV, there's nothing else around you. When your mama comes in and asks why your mouth is open, but you didn't know it was. You're doing something and you don't even know it. If it's something like this, you may be in a trance.

After today's win and all these days picturing the new scarf, sitting down at my weaving table felt so perfect. Deep down, I think Grammy was telling me it was time. That's the last thing I remember.

At some point I grabbed the yarn. Those two beautiful bundles I picked out days ago. I set up the loom and made the warp. I must've been in a trance, because Mama walked in and touched my cheek and I jumped. She scared me. I didn't know she was there. I didn't know I was there. I sorta wasn't.

"I came to check on you and kiss you good night," she said.

I could hear Daddy playing something in the garage. I stared at her, still in a daze. The light from my lamp framed her like a halo. She had pulled her coils into a ponytail on top of her head. She looked like a sister or an aunt, not like my mother. She also looked . . . ghostly. Almost like she wasn't completely here. Fading.

"You were crying," she said, her hand still on my face. But she didn't look worried or surprised.

"Was I?"

"Um-hm." She touched the yarn, which was still stretched across the table. "Does it remind you of Grammy?"

I nodded.

"That just means you loved her. It takes a long time for a sad heart to feel better. Keep going, Jilly. She would be so proud of you. Your creativity. Your courage."

My hands rested on the loom, ready for me to wind the warp and finish the scarf I saw in my mind. I stared again at the yarn. I really didn't remember making the warp. I couldn't see how I would finish it.

"What if I can't weave anymore?"

Mama tickled my chin. "Looks like you can to me. You're halfway done with something." She waved at the loom, but her arm seemed to move in slow motion. Stiff.

"You had a full day today, Jilly. I want you get some rest now."

I yawned and nodded, and she kissed me on the cheek.

"Mama, have you ever seen this?" I showed her an old scrap of paper I found in one of my baskets. At the top of the paper I'd written "Nit." Underneath that I had drawn a triangle with a *W* on each side.

"No, but look at your cute penmanship." She smiled. "You must've been around six or so."

"Why did I spell *knit* wrong?"

"You didn't. That's Nit. She's an Egyptian goddess. Something to do with weaving. Grammy used to talk about her. Let's look it up tomorrow."

I nodded and told her thank you, but I didn't really say why. She smiled and kissed the other cheek. Maybe she already knew.

When she left the room, I pictured her standing with the light shining all around her. She looked like a goddess herself. But a goddess with the Droops. That's what I call it when she looks tired. Her whole face gets sleepy. Gravity pulls down her pretty cheeks. I just hoped she wasn't getting sick.

I didn't go to bed. Not right away. I finished the scarf! It was just as I imagined—shimmery yellow with sparkly swirls of color. I smiled. Maybe somewhere out there, Grammy smiled, too. And even though it was too warm, I draped it over me as I went to sleep.

Today I really did it.

Today I was brave.

CHAPTER TWENTY

William and the Weaver

I slept with my new scarf Friday night, Saturday, and Sunday. I didn't feel ready to show it to Mama until today. She squealed.

"That's beautiful, Jilly Bean. I'm so glad!"

"Do you want to take it for your workshop today?" I asked. My voice was still a little quiet, but less whispery-croaky.

"Me? No, ma'am. You take it. You made it. That's your cape today. Plus it's a cute color pop with those red glasses." She smiled.

"Oh yeah," I said, remembering them. I'd already gotten used to wearing them, so they'd faded into the background. And then I remembered the last time I wore a cape. I wore it for courage then. This one's for love — for Grammy.

"Oh yeah," she echoed me, tickling my chin.

I swung it around my shoulders and pretended to fly around the kitchen until she told me to hurry up and eat so I wouldn't miss the bus.

I wore my yellow cape out of the house, but by the time I got near the bus stop, I rolled it up and put it into my book-bag. Everyone knows you only wear capes in the call of duty, and going to school today was no sweat.

I chatted with Shelby and Marquez on the bus. Shelby told us all about her mom's new job at the CDC. Something about preventing violence. Marquez nodded but didn't smile much. He was quieter than usual, but he wouldn't admit anything was wrong. "Everything's cool" was all he said. I didn't believe him. I wondered how things were going with the spring cleaning, but I didn't ask. Maybe later, when it was just us.

I felt calm, cool, and collected and sorta floated into Jemison and into class. Everything was fine until recess.

I had to go to the bathroom. Ms. W. told me to go ahead and then meet the class outside. When I finished, I noticed our class door was open just a crack. Maybe the caboose forgot to close it. I stepped inside. I could get in trouble for taking too long, but I wanted to hold my scarf for a second. I pulled it out, swung it around my shoulders, and twirled around once, twice, thr—

"What are you doing?"

I almost bumped into a desk at the sound of that voice. Angelic but snippy. More of a demand than a question. William.

I was hot. Not scared. Mad. But it had the same effect.

Silence. I snatched the cape off as fast as I had put it on and shoved it back into my bag.

"What is that?" He reached into the half-open backpack and yanked it out! I wanted to scratch him or bite him or yell. Something.

Too shocked to move, eyes big saucers, jaws locked shut, I watched as he waved it around like a flag. Triumphant. Then it flew out of his hand and drifted to the ground. The bright shimmery swirls screaming against the pale gray floor. I think it wanted to escape. *I* did, that's for sure. I felt my heart beating in my ears. Mad I thought the coast was clear and it wasn't.

"What's this?" He seemed confused. Annoyed.

My cape. My art. My secret, I thought.

He turned his nose up, like it was gross. It wasn't.

I had enough of his foolishness.

"None of your business," I snipped back, hoarse but loud enough. I kept my eyes on the scarf, but I didn't bend down to pick it up.

"Is that a baby blanket?" he had the nerve to ask, moving closer to me, his voice mocking. "I bet you still suck your thumb."

I breathed. Silent. Eyes still down. Waiting.

He reached down as if to snatch it off the floor.

I saw the word in my head fighting to get out. I said it, quiet, but as mean as I could muster. "No."

"No," he said, echoing me.

I didn't speak again or move. I scowled, balling my face so tight I thought it would explode. I stared at my scarf and I waited, wished on my scarf that he would leave us both alone.

And finally, he did.

He left me there, feeling angry. Mad I didn't say enough. Didn't do enough. *Why didn't I say more?* My ears burned, and I swallowed the lump in my throat. Even though I was alone in the room, I still didn't want to cry. Not there.

I balled my fist and forced the tears to stay put for a few seconds more. I held them back through willpower and tight teeth. I wondered if I would crush them. Crush my teeth to dust.

☆

By the time I made it to the playground, I found Marquez sitting on the curb with his book. He didn't seem to be into it, since he was glancing around at other things.

He looked up at me when I got nearby.

"You're making that face," he said.

"Which one?"

"Your jaws are tight. You look calm, but also like a tornado about to swirl around and destroy everything."

I didn't say anything at first. I grabbed the bar and flipped myself around and upside down.

"My mom does that," I said, picturing the once-in-a-blue-moon times when she gets mad.

"What? Swirls and destroys things?"

"Clenches her jaw when she's mad."

"So what gives?"

"William."

"Again?" he asked.

I nodded. But then I looked over and saw him. Serious Marquez. Nudging a rock instead of reading or joking. I remembered he'd been quiet on the bus, too.

"You're doing it," I said.

"What?"

"Making a face."

He didn't deny it, but he didn't explain. "What does it look like?" he asked.

"You know—like when you're in the middle of a logic puzzle and you keep double-checking your work to see whatcha missed?"

"Yeah."

"So is it a puzzle?" I asked.

He thought about it for a minute. He looked at the school, almost as if he thought the answer was on the roof or the wall or something. "Sorta," he said finally. "I almost figured it out. Just gotta make him understand. He comes around and . . . I don't know—" He shrugged. "It's better when he's *not* around."

"Your dad?"

"Yeah. It's a long story."

"I don't mind." I got off the bar and sat beside him on the curb.

He exhaled. "He wants to get back with Moms. Except. Well, she don't smile when he's around. They just no good for each other. When it's just him, me, and my sister, he's great. But with her? I don't know, man, he's someone else. Ever since I was little. I'm always the one making her laugh, cheering her up."

"Oh." I nodded. "She smiles with her new boyfriend?"

"Mr. Mathew? All the time. He's gonna be my stepdad soon. He's cool."

"Wooow! That's why your dad gotta get his stuff!"

"Yeah. He doesn't know yet."

"She won't tell him?"

"She tried. He got mad. She got mad. It's dumb."

He shook his head, annoyed, remembering.

I pointed to the bars. "Wanna hang?"

He nodded. We got on and flipped upside down, swaying in silence until it was time to go back inside.

CHAPTER TWENTY-ONE
Champions Never Say Die

Marquez smiles every day. His right dimple sinks into his cheek. White teeth peek out from behind braces with bright blue bands.

When he smiles, you smile. Everyone does. You can't help it. His whole face glows, including his eyes, and he lights up everything around him. Even Ms. W. has to catch herself because she will smile when he is smiling. But when he smiles in class, it usually means mischief.

Today there were no bright blue bands. No gleaming teeth. No dimple. Even his eyes were quiet.

He usually sat near the middle of the bus, stirring up silliness. But today he sat near the front. I slipped in beside him.

"Why so quiet today?" I asked. "Same puzzle?"

Like yesterday, it took him a long time to say. Like the answer was hidden in a maze he had to walk first. I waited the way Ms. W. would. I waited and watched. To see if he would smile. To see if that dimple would say hello. He did not. His dimple did not. He looked at me with those quiet black-brown eyes and pressed his lips up in a pretend smile. More like a grimace.

Finally, he answered me.

"Same puzzle. Same battle to make my dad understand." he said. "Gotta train."

I stared at him, into his eyes.

"But how?"

"Well, I gotta practice what to say."

"That's not too bad. You can practice with me."

"It's more than that," he said, lowering his voice. "I don't want him to get mad at me."

We stared at each other.

"How does training help?" I asked, matching his volume.

"When I do it right, it helps me feel . . . less scared. So I won't chicken out."

I nodded.

"Keeps your heart strong," I said. "I get it now."

He nodded back.

"You can do it," I told him. I really believed it.

Then I told him what I had been thinking. That he was wrong about something from before. I hold my breath when I am nervous, and he held his breath then, waiting for me to explain.

"Remember you said the winners in history are champions? The ones who overcome the odds?"

He nodded.

"That's not right," I said. "The champions are the ones who try to fight at all."

He didn't react at first. But then I saw the dimple. Or the shadow, at least. His mouth didn't smile, but his eyes did. Then he flipped it on me.

"What about you?" he asked. "Are you a champion?"

"I don't know," I said, looking at my lap.

"Maybe?"

"Yeah, maybe."

☆

Today is day fourteen. It's a candling day. The chicks should hatch in seven more days! The ones who are still living, anyway. Inside the oval today, the embryo is moving to turn its head into the butt end of the egg. The rounder part. That's where the air cell is.

Chickens have three eyelids, which seems sort of gross to me. They've all been growing, and today the eye is covered. If we could really see the inside of an egg, we'd think the embryo looks like a chick now. There's even downy fuzz all over its body. But it needs those last seven days to finish developing. If the egg cracked open now, it would die.

Ms. W. covered the windows with bulletin board paper again. When we were ready to candle the eggs, she warned us that it was a counting day. No counting chicks *before* they hatched, but at some point, you had to count them *out*. If it was obvious they weren't alive, we would have to discard the eggs. Ten out of twelve had looked good when we last checked. Who knew what we would find this time? I tried not to worry.

We pulled our chairs near the incubator and sat very quiet and still. I don't think anyone even breathed. No one begged to hold the eggs this time. We all wanted Ms. W. to do it, with our hands a safe distance away.

She selected eggs from the incubator, going in the same order as before. She took each egg one by one and placed it on the candler. She invited the pairs for a closer look, but no one dared.

The first few looked great. Each time she picked one out, we got nervous all over again and waited for her reaction. Then she picked up one of the blanks—mine. I gripped my chair. Scottie did the same.

She flicked the light on and cooed. It was growing! We cheered as loud as the first goal in a soccer game. "See, she's just a late bloomer," Ms. W. said, smiling. She looked relieved, but not as much as I felt.

A few moments later we saw that the other blank was still a blank. Two girls sniffled at the news. That was the one they'd claimed from the beginning. We all felt a little down. Ms. W. waited for them to stop crying before she went on.

But that wasn't the end of it. Ms. W. did the next few, which all looked good. And then she candled the last egg, one that looked great a few days ago. But this time when she flicked on the light, she gasped. Her shoulders drooped low. We knew something went horribly wrong. She pointed. Fearing for something we could not really imagine, we stood, wringing hands, biting fingers, leaning forward to see what had happened.

Inside the egg was a thin ring, a blood ring. It meant something wasn't quite right inside, and the embryo had died.

Ms. W.'s voice was barely above a whisper when she said it must be discarded. This one and the blank. We had to take them out so they wouldn't explode later and compromise the whole hatch.

"Should . . . should we hold a funeral?" Marquez asked.

We all looked at him.

No smiles. No dimple. He stared at the last egg, now cradled in Ms. W.'s hand. "You know what I mean," he said. "We should say nice things for a few minutes."

"What do you all think about that?" Ms. W. asked the class.

Everyone nodded.

We went around one by one, and you could say something if you wanted. Rashida, William, Janice, and Shelby all said something. And Marquez, too. I wanted to reach out and squeeze his hand. My hand drifted in his direction. But he didn't notice, so I let it drift back to my lap. I didn't like seeing him quiet or sad, or whatever he was these days.

One or two others spoke, but most of us didn't say anything. I didn't either. Ms. W. placed the egg back on the candler for now and checked the incubator settings. It was time for us to pack up for the day. She said she would take care of everything once we were gone. We dragged the chairs back to our desks and gathered our things to go. The dismissal bell rang.

Out of the Dirty Dozen, we're officially down to ten.

CHAPTER TWENTY-TWO
I've Got the Power

Maybe it's because the late bloomer bloomed. Or maybe it was the blood ring. Either way, I woke up ready to try something a little different for today's round of the Mind Bender. I didn't want big and twisty hair or ponytails. I wanted to wear my hair like a ballerina, with a bun on top.

I got dressed as fast as I could and started doing my hair. Mama had to help me finish it because my bun was lopsided and I had strands flying everywhere.

"It's not even a Monday moon day, and here you are doing something brand new," Mama said, looking sharp in a white dress and matching heels. She had another workshop today. This one was with women executives, so she wanted to look the part. She pulled on her robe to make sure she stayed pristine while she did my hair. As pretty as she was, I noticed she seemed to be moving in slow motion. Maybe she's been working too hard lately. Daddy said stress isn't good for lupus. I hoped she could relax soon.

"Yeah. Today feels like a bun day," I said.

"Good for you," said Mama. "You don't need any excuses to be yourself, Jilly . . . Voilà!" With that, she passed me the mirror. "You like?" she asked.

"I like. Thanks, Mama!" I said, smiling to the reflection.

I took a couple of bites of my waffles, and then I got an idea.

"I have to get something out of my room," I called over my shoulder, running upstairs to grab my scarf. After the William thing, I'd come home and taken it out of my bag. But it was Mind Bender day. Hair buns, brains, and a yellow cape. I flung it around my shoulders and ran back to the kitchen.

"Oh. Superhero today?" Mama asked, noticing my new accessory.

"Yep!"

"Well, I hope that cape can help you fly through breakfast. Because you're running out of time."

"You always say that."

"It's always true." She smiled.

"Not always!"

"Well. Mostly." We laughed, and I hurried. As usual.

☆

Never in my ten years of life have I ever heard of the power going out at school. Yet there we were, in the middle of the day, with no power. We all laughed at first and heard some kids in other rooms screaming. But Ms. W. wasn't laughing. She looked at the ceiling—at the darkened lights and then at the incubator that was now off.

Shelby was the first to get it. "The chickens!"

All eyes went to the incubator. Ms. W. tried to calm us down, but she didn't look very relaxed to me. "They'll be okay if it's just out for a little while," she said.

No one believed it. School power *never* goes out! Who knew how long it might take?

"Think about it," she said. "The hen doesn't sit on the eggs all day with no break. She gets up, stretches her legs. Eats, uses the bathroom, that sort of thing." We giggled at chickens using the bathroom. But it was nervous giggles, and Ms. W. had not cracked a smile.

"Did anyone bring a jacket to school?" she asked. Everyone shook their heads no, because it was late April in Georgia and we all knew it would be warm by recess. I shook my head no with everyone else, not really thinking. That is, until William cleared his throat. In a singsongy voice he announced, "Why don't you ask Jillian?"

I had no idea why he did that. I scowled. I could make out his smirk in the shadows. But then I remembered—my cape.

Ms. W. looked at me, surprised or maybe confused, or both. "You have a jacket, Jillian?"

"It's not a jacket, but yes, I have something. I have a—something we can use."

"Get it, please, if you don't mind."

"Okay."

I pushed back my chair, which sounded loud in the quiet room. Everyone watched as I shuffled away from my seat near the window and into the darkest part of the room, back to our cubbies and hooks. My cheeks burned from all the eyes on me. I wished my scarf would just magic itself to the incubator instead of this big reveal. I pulled it out, rolled up in a neat cylinder now, and presented it to Ms. W.

She peered through her golden glasses, warming up her x-ray vision. Slowly she unrolled it, then nodded. I could tell she understood that it was special.

"Wow," she said, inspecting it. "What great fortune we have that you brought this to school today. This looks handmade. Did someone give it to you?"

My ears were burning now. And those cheerful colors made my head hurt. Even in the half-dark room, the sparkly swirls seemed so loud. I looked at my feet, at my plain white sneakers. She waited for my answer.

"I made it."

I heard but ignored the *ohhhs* and whispers. I was embarrassed enough by the attention. I didn't want to hear anybody making fun of my *something*.

"My grandmother taught me how to weave," I added, feeling very sad saying it aloud. I kept my eyes down, praying I wouldn't have to say more.

"Another hidden talent," she said. "Well, the chicks will be grateful, I'm sure."

Shelby yelled, pointing at the teacher, "You called them chicks! They haven't hatched!"

Ms. W. waved her off, saying, "My bad! You're right, of course."

We all laughed at her slang. Even me.

"Help me spread it out?" she asked me, smiling. "We want to keep them warm but make sure they get enough air," she explained, adjusting it so it didn't smother the incubator. "We should be fine, everyone. The lights probably won't be off long, but we want to make sure."

After the red ring yesterday, no one wanted to take any chances.

"Thanks for sharing your beautiful work, Jillian," said Ms. W. Then she peered over her glasses and winked.

The lights were out for only another hour or so, which is forever in elementary school time. Long enough that they decided to reschedule the next Mind Bender round for tomorrow.

I had another day to train my heart.

☆

The whole day was off schedule, but we still had some time for recess. The entire fifth grade was outside, but there was more talking, less playing. Even the jump ropers were only half into it.

"Do you want to jump today?" Rashida asked, eyeing the small group.

I shook my head. "I can just watch."

"That's no fun! What if I teach you our routine? Come over here."

I followed her until we found a spot alone.

With her usual confidence, she got right down to business. She counted and snapped to her own beat, one-two-three-four, and began dancing a short routine.

"Can you dance?" she asked, still grooving.

I nodded, hoping she wouldn't ask me to do it. I didn't really want to dance out there in front of everyone, but she didn't seem to notice. By her third time doing the routine, her confidence was contagious, and I decided to give it a try. She never once laughed at me. She just kept going until I got the hang of it.

"Okay, now jump!" She repeated the routine again, dancing, snapping, and then jumping, too!

That was too much. I laughed so hard, I threw her off beat.

"How can you do all of that together?" I asked.

"Practice!" she said, out of breath from jumping and giggling at the same time. "Just practice when you get home."

"Where did you learn that?"

"YouTube! They have TikTok mash-ups and tutorials of everything. My mother would have a fit if she knew."

"Really? Why?"

"I told you—decorum." The giggles disappeared, and she leaned toward me.

"It's because of my aunt. My mom's sister is really artistic. She even belly-dances!" She whispered that last part.

"What's wrong with that?"

"Nothing! But my mom doesn't want us to be like that when we grow up. She wants me and my sister to be"—she thought for a moment—"serious. Professional. So we dress up every day and make hundreds on everything and behave in school. No funky clothes. No wild dances."

"Oh." I nodded. "I'll try to practice." I pictured Mama teaching about moons. Was that professional? Daddy and his rock band, Grammy and her red lipstick. I don't think any of that is serious. It's fun, though.

Everyone wants to be like Rashida, but it sounds like Rashida just wants to be . . . free.

☆

Mama still seemed to be moving in slow motion when she got home from work. But she perked up when I whooshed around the kitchen wearing my scarf like a cape.

"I am Wonder Woman. I saved the day!"

Mama giggled, then said, "You know, I don't know how much she wears a cape, Jilly Bean. And where are your boots and bracelets?"

"That's okay. I am Wonder Woman, and therefore I can dress however I want!"

"Now we're talking." Mama nodded, a huge smile on her droopy face. "You're cheerful. Good day?"

"Yes. I really saved the day!" I told her all about my scarf/ cape keeping the eggs warm until the power came on.

"See?" said Mama. "Weaving is magic after all. This calls for a celebration."

"We're celebrating?" asked Daddy, coming home just in time to catch the news.

"Yes! I saved the developing chicks with my trusty cape! With my heroic weaving."

"Heroic, indeed," he said. "How shall we celebrate?"

"Dance party!" I yelled.

"Coming right up," he said, leading the way to the back- yard. "You okay to dance?" he asked Mama. "We don't want to overdo anything."

"I'm fine, I'm fine!" she said, waving away his question. "I just need to kick off these heels, finally."

Out we went into the late afternoon sun and danced and sang Lenny and Beyoncé songs. I forgot my Mama can shake it. She really got down in her dress and bare feet. I even tried out Rashida's new routine a couple of times. We laughed and laughed. It was my favorite day in a long time.

After a few songs Mama headed back inside. "All right y'all," she said, waving good-bye. "I've had enough fun."

"Aww," Daddy and I said, trying to keep her outside a little while longer.

"I'm tired. It's been a long few weeks. I'm going to drink a little water and cool off."

Daddy eyed her—like maybe he was worried—but she smiled and shooed him away. We danced to one more song, then came inside to make dinner.

CHAPTER TWENTY-THREE

Let Love Rule

Woke up early, excited for another chance at Mind Bender. I was still nervous, but I felt ready. May Day was twelve days away, and even though I still worried about what people thought, I wasn't hiding anymore. My heart didn't hurt so much. The way Ms. W. looked at my scarf yesterday made my stomach lurch. In a good way. I felt proud to cover the eggs with something I made. It showed me that maybe it was okay to do my own thing. Really. With my hair and clothes and my ideas. Maybe the Mind Bender would be okay, too.

I didn't need to *try* to be different from everyone — or the same, either. I could just do what seemed right to me. Today a ponytail felt right. A high ponytail with twist across the front. I did my hair, then put on jeans and a T-shirt. I went to the kitchen humming "Let Love Rule," from last night's dance party.

"Mama?" My heart stopped when I saw her slumped against the counter. She looked so small. So yellow. Just, all the wrong color and shape and size. "Mommy!" I said, shouting down the shock.

"Daddy!" I yelled at the top of my lungs. I had no idea where he was. "Daddy! Daddy!" I heard his bounding feet, and then I saw him.

He wasted no time with questions. He saw Mama crumpled, slumped, sick. "I knew it," he said quietly. Almost angry, but I didn't know why.

I watched him shift from the laughing, singing Daddy from last night to a serious, scowling Dad this morning. He filled a glass of water and encouraged her to drink it, rubbing her back.

"You can feed yourself, right, Jillian?"

I flinched. He never calls me Jillian.

"Instant oatmeal? Juice? I'm taking Mama to the doctor," he said.

"I'm not hungry," I said, feeling empty. Shocked. I plopped down in a chair, staring at the two of them.

"What time does your bus come?" he asked. "Go ahead and ride the bus to school. You can eat breakfast there, right?"

"What's wrong with Mommy?"

"Just tired, baby," she whispered. "And a little achy."

"Jillian," he said for the second time. I was really scared then. He stared at me, my sad eyes filling with tears. He clenched his jaw. "Will you grab my keys and open the door?"

I scrambled to do what he asked. I was very glad for my jeans and sneakers. I felt serious and ready for action.

Daddy scooped Mama up in his arms as if she were a little girl, and headed out the door. He called over his shoulder, "Grab her wallet, please."

I snatched it from her purse and also grabbed my yellow scarf draped across a kitchen chair. I rushed to the garage, jumped into the back seat on the driver's side.

"Jillian." Third time.

"Daddy, no. I can't go to school."

He looked at me then, jaw still tight, face all pinched and frowny. I sniffed all hints of tears away, so he'd see I was brave.

"I wanna go where you guys are going."

He shook his head ever so slightly, but then he announced, sounding unsure, "Okay, baby. Let's go." He punched the button on the remote and opened the garage door.

"We're going to the doctor?" I asked, buckling my seat belt. I wanted to make sure he wouldn't try to take me to school after all.

"Yes, to the emergency room. If it's nothing serious, we can just come back home and take the rest of the day off." He tried to say it like *if they're out of chocolate ice cream, we'll just come back,* but it didn't work. He sounded tense and sad. He sounded the way I felt. Scared.

He leaned Mama back in her seat. I held her hand and draped the scarf across her. It wouldn't be like when Grammy died. She would come back home. Right?

"Don't worry, Jilly Bean," Mama whispered. Maybe she knew what I was thinking. But I *was* worried. I saw her face balled up, the way it looks when you're in pain and you won't say so.

Daddy started the car and touched her cheek. He still looked angry, or maybe he was in pain, too.

He backed out and we sped off.

CHAPTER TWENTY-FOUR

The ER

When we got to the ER, five or six people sat in the waiting room, but it was nothing like TV. No ambulances roaring in. No bloody people being rolled and rushed this way and that. No shouting. I saw a few worried faces, a man holding his side and moaning, a woman holding an ice pack to a little boy's wrist. People looked unhappy, but not deathly ill. It made me feel a teeny bit better.

Daddy strode up to the window with Mama in his arms. The receptionist rushed him to the back so a triage nurse could assess her. I followed close behind.

The nurse asked her a few questions and took a few notes. A doctor came in next.

Right away they decided to admit her to the hospital. They suspected it had something to do with Mama's lupus. She needed to stay for at least one night while they ran tests and gave her medicine to help her feel better. Daddy helped her onto one of those rolling beds — a gurney — and other nurses wheeled her back to a small room.

The triage nurse returned the scarf to me. "Don't worry. You can give it back to her once she's settled in her hospital room," she said.

For now Daddy and I held all her things — her wedding ring and earrings, her wallet and the scarf. We followed her to the temporary room and sat down in hard chairs.

Daddy's face was tight, like Marquez's. Like mine. Like everyone's when they are worried and not sure what to do. No one said anything at first. Then Mama said she wanted to take a nap.

Daddy barked a laugh, more like a cough. "Of course," he said.

I squeezed his hand, and he turned his face to me. I am not sure his eyes saw me at all. "I'll take you to school," he said.

"No, Daddy. I don't want to go." He nodded and went back to staring at Mama.

Nurses rushed around, hooking her up to things. Murmuring to each other and taking notes.

"Ready?" A friendly looking nurse leaned in, all set to direct us to Mama's room. It was a sad parade, me and Daddy following behind a doctor and two nurses who were pushing Mama down a long white corridor.

Her hospital room was cold but busy. Daddy and I sat on

a cushiony bench near Mama's bed. Nurses hooked her up to more things. Wrote more notes. They talked to Mama, who was groggy but awake. They monitored numbers on machines and stuck her with things. Sometimes they talked to Daddy.

The whole time, I sat very still. Very quiet. It was easy to blend in. Natural. Normal. Something was familiar. This place. This feeling.

"Are you scared?" one nurse asked me.

Scared and sad. Grammy went to the hospital last spring and never came home. It couldn't be good that Mama was getting sick so close to May Day. But I didn't want to say or think about any of that.

I shook my head no.

"Good," she said. "Your mom is going to be just fine."

A few minutes later another one smiled at me. "Look at you, pretty girl, being so quiet for your mom. That's a good girl. Let her rest." She patted my hand.

When the coast was clear, I put the scarf on her again. The shimmery swirls looked pretty against her honey-brown skin.

As the morning went on, Daddy got his color back. His breathing moved deeper in his chest. By the time the doctor announced we could go home tomorrow if Mama continued to do well today, I thought Daddy might hum. He settled for a small smile.

Then the doctor turned to me. "Do you have any questions?" He stood still, waiting. I shook my head no.

That was a lie. I wanted to know why we were here. Why Mama was laid out with tubes, sleeping in a hospital bed.

"Nothing?" he asked again. I didn't answer. I saw the words in my head, a cloud of letters like a billboard in my brain. But they were too big. They couldn't travel down into my mouth, so I couldn't get them out. I just watched them floating there. I thought I had gotten better at shrinking the letters. The ones that started off far too big for my mouth.

"Jilly?"

I looked up into my daddy's brown eyes. I think he saw the letters swirling. He rubbed my cheeks and coaxed them out.

"Why?" I whispered. "Why are we here?" I don't cry in public, so I did not let tears leave my eyes. But they were there, two pools of water standing still. My face remained dry, but I couldn't risk saying anything else.

The doctor asked if I knew that Mama has lupus. I nodded yes. He explained that being in the sun could be toxic for some people with the disease. Mama had already been a little worn down, and yesterday's celebration in the sun triggered a chain reaction in her body. A flare.

I stared at him, understanding, but it didn't feel like understanding. I was pulled into swirling tunnel, remembering.

"Jilly?" Daddy tried calling me from the tunnel.

"I'm not trying to scare you," said the doctor, sounding unsure. I stared at his badge, but his name didn't stick.

"I'm not scared," I said to the badge. Except I think I said it inside myself. Looking around this tunnel of memories, I saw myself small and sitting on Daddy's lap. I saw Mama in the hospital with the tubes. I saw the nurses giving me treats, saying I was being good because I was quiet. I saw me trying even harder to blend in and be quiet while Mama got better.

I felt a coolness by my side. I blinked. Daddy and the doctor had left the room. Daddy returned alone, looking almost like himself.

"You ready to go home while Mommy sleeps?" he asked.

"We've been here? Before?"

"Ah. You remember that?"

"Kinda." I nodded. "I don't remember what was wrong. But everyone said nice things to me because I was quiet. Because I was invisible."

He looked at me, falling into his own tunnel of memories. His eyes got that faraway look.

"Like the nurse just said I was good and quiet," I said. "No one explained what was wrong with Mommy, just that I was good to be so quiet. I was a good girl, like a magic trick."

He kissed my hand and held it. "Sometimes adults do

that. When we're upset about something, we don't do a good job of telling kids what's happening, or letting kids be themselves."

I nodded again.

"Adults think kids can't handle the truth, so we tell" — he hesitated — "only parts of it. Then we run around and figure things out."

I thought adults already had things figured out. They don't. I didn't know if that made me feel better or worse.

"I'm sorry you felt invisible. Or felt you *should* be invisible. You never have to be invisible for me. Or your mom. Not at school either."

Mama stirred then. After we kissed her hello, she looked down and saw the scarf on her chest. She smiled. "You should weave more often. You're so creative, Jilly Bean. You have so much to offer." She yawned. "Don't keep it to yourself."

She took a deep breath then, and sighed.

"Mommy, are you okay? You want the doctor?"

"I'm fine, baby," she said. "I'm just . . . very sleepy." She yawned again and fell asleep.

But her face was smoother this time. She wasn't frowned up. She wasn't in pain.

☆

By late afternoon Ms. Sandy came to pick me up. She doubled as the neighborhood grandma and candy lady. She had long silver hair she wore braided down her back. She said her mother was Black and Cherokee and her daddy was Mexican. I just know that she baby-sat all the neighborhood kids, and folded you into bear hugs that smelled like vanilla and cinnamon.

Daddy wrote me a note for school and said he would stay at the hospital with Mama.

"We'll be back by the time you get home from school tomorrow," he promised.

I nodded and kissed them both goodbye. Mama smiled. She looked a little better. Not as yellow. Not as small.

Even though I was probably too old, I was glad Ms. Sandy held my hand on the long walk to the car.

I fell asleep almost as soon as we got home. I love Ms. Sandy's cooking, but I was sleepy, not hungry. I planned to take a nap and eat dinner later, but I didn't wake up until morning.

CHAPTER TWENTY-FIVE
The Sky Is Falling

Ms. Sandy woke me up just before the alarm.

"Wake up, mija," she said into my ear.

I yawned, stirring, remembering Mama in the hospital.

"Your daddy called," she said softly. "Mama's doing well. They wish you to have a good day. Let's get it started, yes?"

I nodded and yawned, but after she left, I stayed put, snuggled under the covers. I thought about what happened. The nurses saying nice things. Daddy saying I didn't have to blend in. I didn't have to be invisible. A few days ago Mama said I didn't need excuses to be myself. I don't have to make any decisions because of anyone else. Maybe that's what Mama means about pointing at things "out there" with all your other fingers pointing back at you.

"Jillian?" Ms. Sandy peeked back inside my room. "Are you up? You didn't fall back asleep, did you?"

"No, ma'am. I'm getting up." I yawned again. I felt strange, like I was forgetting something. At the same time, I felt hopeful, like everything would be okay today. Like Mama would be smiling later.

I got dressed in a hurry—jeans and a T-shirt again. I parted my hair down the middle and made little balls like Minnie Mouse ears. Mama couldn't help me today, so I did my best to make sure my part was straight. I couldn't shake the feeling that I was forgetting something, but I didn't have time to sit still and figure it out. Dressed and ready to go, I hurried downstairs.

Ms. Sandy made grits! The good kind. Salty and buttery and thick. And eggs scrambled with cheese and chorizo. It was delicious, but I'm sorta grossed out about eating eggs now.

"Don't worry about your mommy, okay, mija?" she said as I was finishing breakfast. "Your daddy says they might even be home before you. And don't forget your note for being absent."

I nodded, and she hugged me goodbye, smelling like vanilla and cinnamon, even in the morning. I smiled, breathed her in, and waved goodbye. Off to the bus stop I went.

Little Lonna pointed at me when I got there. "You look like Minnie Mouse," she said. I waved at her and smiled.

I still couldn't remember what I'd forgotten, but so far, so good.

☆

Marquez wasn't on the bus. He's never absent. Shelby sat in her usual spot, toward the middle. And did I imagine it? Or did she give me a strange look?

I wasn't imagining. By the time I got to class, there were more looks and now bees buzzing. Rashida put an end to all that. She walked right up to me and asked, "Did you lose your voice again?"

Suddenly I was worried that "so far, so good" had gone as far as it could. She looked shocked or confused, or something I didn't recognize. Her face, usually calm, cool, and collected, looked more like a raisin—wrinkly. Over her shoulder I spotted Marquez walking in.

"Not . . . Why?" I reached inside my bookbag and froze.

"Oh, no," I said to my bag. There was no cape inside. I felt panicky. Maybe that's what I'd forgotten.

Marquez and Shelby came over, and the three of them all huddled around me. Eyeing me with the same sad confusion, as if they didn't know what to say. Marquez looked shy! Like he didn't want to meet my eyes. To make matters worse, there was William. I could never ignore him properly, and there he was in the background, yelling in my direction. "Oh, you're back!" It sounded like he was trying to be mean, but it came out . . . sad.

"What's going on?" I asked my classmates. They wouldn't say anything. Just stood there with those strange looks on their faces. Then Ms. W. called me.

"Jillian could you come here, please?" Not over to her desk. Outside the classroom. My stomach lurched like when I'm riding Acrophobia at Six Flags. I went into the hallway with her, and she closed the door behind us.

"Ma'am?" I said, looking up at her.

"What happened yesterday?" She looked down at me, staring hard through those golden glasses. I felt like an ant under a magnifying glass in the sun.

I swallowed, nervous. "My mom got sick. We were at the hospital all day." I remembered Daddy's note and pulled it out of my pocket. "Here." I passed it to her.

"Hospital? Is she okay?" She read it quickly and looked at me again.

"Yeah, she has lupus, and the doctor said she got too much sun. Anyway, it was an emergency. Did I miss a big—" Before I could get the words out, I finally remembered. The thing I kept forgetting.

"Mind Bender," we said at the same time. Only she said it in a concerned whisper and I said it like homework I forgot to turn in.

"Yes," she said. "I'm afraid it was yesterday. We selected finalists for the Big League round." I stared at her, disbelieving. "Rashida scored highest, and Kyle from Mrs. Fueyo's class next."

I missed it, I thought. *I missed my chance to show Grammy I could be confident in myself. To just be Jillian, wearing colors and*

cool hairstyles and competing in the biggest competition in school.
Deep down, I thought I even had a chance to win.

What do you do when you feel everything at once? I felt sad and relieved and shocked and disappointed. It all jumbled around inside of me. A big storm cloud rolling in the middle of a sunny summer day.

"Oh," I finally said. And then, nothing worked. Not biting my tongue or balling up my fists. Not telling myself to hold it in. Not swallowing the jumble back down.

The storm cloud opened up, and tears rushed from my eyes and rolled down my cheeks. Ms. W. hugged me, squeezing me tight. And I cried all my tears into her. At school. In the hallway. What else was there to do? I finally trained my heart to try, and now it's too late.

"I'm proud of you," she said. "I know you're shy. But you were willing to face your fears. To be yourself. That means a lot."

It didn't feel like a lot. It felt the same as always. Bitter. Someone else will taste the chocolate at the end.

"Jillian, you might not believe it yet, but you really are brave." She paused, her hands resting on my shoulders.

I nodded, looking at the floor.

She told me to drink some water and wash my face. "Come back in when you're ready."

I stayed in the bathroom until my eyes looked clear, then I walked back to my seat without seeing anyone or anything.

I sat quietly the whole morning. Wondered if Mama was home. Wondered why I ever thought I should try to be the Mind Bender champion.

I didn't try to blend in, but I did hope, at least for this morning, that I was invisible after all.

CHAPTER TWENTY-SIX
Egg-ceptional

Marquez sat next to me during lunch. Shelby sat on his other side. Between bites of cold cheese pizza, he asked me what happened. I told him about my mom and what Ms. W. said in the hall. That I was out.

"What did you say?" he asked.

"Nothing." I didn't mention the crying.

He took another bite. "Tell her you want another chance," he said, his mouth full of pizza. "Ask for a special round or something."

"You can't do that."

"You *can* do that. It might not work, but you can ask."

"But Ms. W. didn't say—"

"It ain't up to her! You know what Ms. W. did say? She said don't count your chickens before they hatch. Don't count them in or out. You counting yourself out!"

"Everything ain't like a history book, Marquez." I rolled

my eyes. A few people looked at us. He didn't seem to notice.

"It ain't about books!" he said, matching my tone. "It's the *people*. They don't leave it up to other folks. You can't help it your mama got sick."

Rashida squeezed in across from us.

"What are you two down here fussing about?" She sounded like a mom.

"What Jillian should do about being disqualified. Her moms went to the hospital yesterday."

Rashida gasped. "Is that what happened? Is she okay?"

"Yeah. She has . . ." I trailed off. I never really talked about Mama like this, and I wasn't sure what they'd think. Rashida and Marquez looked worried. They wanted to know.

"She has something called lupus," I said. "Sometimes her immune system attacks itself."

"Oh, I know about things like that," said Rashida, nodding like she really did know.

"You do?" I asked, surprised.

"Yeah. My sister, Valerie."

"She has lupus?"

"No, sickle cell," said Rashida. "Some of her blood cells are shaped funny. Sometimes she doesn't feel well, and she has to go to the hospital for a couple of days."

"Oh," I said.

"She's okay now. But sometimes it just flares up."

"Well, my Mama should be home when I get out of school," I said. I hoped.

"It's not fair," chimed in Shelby. "You shouldn't be out just because your mom was sick. You had the next highest score, after Rashida."

"I agree. Let's do something about it," said Rashida. "Let's ask for an exception. See if we can redo the last round. Or *something*."

Shelby, Marquez, and I just stared at her.

"What? Why are you all looking at me that way?" she asked.

"Let's?" I ask.

"I'm the reigning champion. I still have the highest score this year. I know excellence when I see it." She smiled then. "Besides, we're friends, aren't we? Seems like a friend would want to help you."

Wow. Friends? Wow. I'm sure Mama would've told me to close my mouth so the flies wouldn't get in. I didn't know what to say.

"Well?" Rashida asked.

I nodded, my stormy insides suddenly feeling rays of sunshine.

"I never thought to ask for an exception," I said. "To be exceptional."

"Don't you mean egg-ceptional?"

We groaned at Marquez.

"Y'all don't think it's too late?" I asked. I didn't want to get my hopes up.

"If the Mind Bender ain't over," said Marquez, "you still got plenty of time."

Everyone around the table nodded. I pushed my glasses up on my nose and sat up straight, thinking about what to do. By the time we made it to recess, I still wasn't sure.

☆

"Today's a big day, everyone," Ms. W. announced when it was time for science. "We're getting ready for the final stretch."

Today, inside the eggs, the almost-chicks are wrapped inside the membrane. The air cell is still growing larger, and now they can use the bathroom. I couldn't really imagine having to go in that small space. Ms. W. tried to explain where the waste goes. She showed us a picture, but we all just said "eww" and "yuck!" As gross as that was, it wasn't the worst part.

The almost-chicks are still absorbing the yolk and *their own guts*! So gross and impossible to picture. Everything outside must be sucked inside. Only then can they hatch. Ms. W. says it's *vital*. They must absorb their guts or they will die. I'm still not sure why their intestines are outside their bodies anyway, but I didn't wanna ask.

"I'm putting this inside the incubator today," Ms. W.

announced, holding up a dark brown mat. I think she just wanted to change the subject. We had all turned a little green.

"They're getting new carpet?" asked Jake. We chuckled.

"Not exactly. It's a nonslip surface," Ms. W. explained. "They'll be a little stumbly when they hatch, and we don't want them to slip and fall. This will help a little."

"Oh! It's a yoga mat!" yelled Marquez. We laughed for real that time, and Ms. W. nodded her head.

"Sort of like that. Except the chicks won't be doing many poses. Anyway, I'm adjusting their water so they will have more humidity and oxygen. It'll be like they're at the beach."

"Why do they need more humidity?" asked William.

"Their membranes need to stay moist. Otherwise the chick may be trapped and unable to get out."

My eyes got big. Being a chick was gross *and* dangerous.

"All right, time is running out. Y'all ready?" Ms. W. asked.

I could see everyone stiffen up. Ms. W. wanted to candle the eggs one more time. A last look before the hatch. But after the red ring last time, everyone felt a little nervous. A few of my classmates went up to check on their eggs, but not everyone.

All the eggs looked good. No egg funerals. No tears.

The incubator has turned the chicks a little each day, but Ms. W. will keep them still from now on. The chicks are turning on their own — *inside* the eggs! They have to get themselves in the right position to hatch. How in the world do they know which end is the right end? I wonder if they are ever worried or scared they will do something wrong.

CHAPTER TWENTY-SEVEN
Suck It Up

Mama really was there when I got home from school Friday afternoon, but she slept until bedtime. She was wearing the scarf I made. Daddy said she told the nurses about her superhero cape every time she woke up. She slept most of the day Saturday, but she was feeling better. By Sunday, she was bored and chatty. She asked me about school.

"How are the chicks doing?" she asked. "Catch Mama up."

"They're good! They're hatching in a few more days. We looked at them Friday, but that's it. Now we wait," I said. "No more touching or moving them around. Ms. W. says just patience and love."

"That sounds like a good recipe for most things." Mama smiled. "So the chicks are done growing? They're fully developed now and just waiting to hatch?"

"Almost. But the gross part is their intestines! Their guts are on the outside of them. They have to suck the rest of the yolk and their guts inside."

"Really? I never knew that." Mama sounded in awe and a little grossed out at the same time.

"They need to have everything inside to be ready to break free."

I stared at the sparkly scarf. The first thing I'd weaved since Grammy died. It felt good to be weaving again, even if it was only one thing so far. Maybe we could go to Keet's for some new yarn when Mama felt better.

"Whatcha thinking, Jilly Bean?"

"Does it hurt?"

"Does what hurt, baby?"

"Sucking in the gut. Getting ready to break out of the shell."

She seemed to think about this for a moment. "I don't think that part is painful," she said finally. "It's difficult. But it just happens naturally. Getting out of the egg is another thing, though. That's where the real work comes in."

"Yeah."

"It's probably tiring. I imagine it's pretty scary, too. But either they remain stuck inside that egg or . . ."

"They pip, unzip, and escape!"

Mama giggled. "What's that?"

"We learned it in school. Pip is when they break the first holes in the shell. And unzip is when they make their own zipper, when they poke holes all around the shell."

She nodded. Maybe she could picture a chick breaking

free. I didn't tell Mama that I think I have pipped, but have not quite unzipped myself from my shell. I looked once more at the yellow scarf. Nine days till May Day. Maybe tomorrow I will request an egg-ception after all.

CHAPTER TWENTY-EIGHT
Signs of Life

Monday, moon day. On the bus, I told Marquez and Shelby I'd made up my mind. I was going to ask for the exception. To ask Ms. W. if we could redo the Mind Bender round I missed. When we got to class, they gave me The Look.

I raised my hand to get her attention.

"Yes, Ms. Jillian?" When I hesitated, she called me to her desk. Everyone was busy with morning work, except for Shelby and Marquez, who just pretended to be busy. Rashida kept her eyes on her paper, but I saw her flash a small thumbs-up.

"I have a question," I said, more to the desk than to the teacher.

"Yes, what is it?"

I stood up straighter and raised my eyes to meet hers. "It's about Mind Bender."

She nodded, waiting for me to continue.

"I know I missed it, but . . ."

She raised her eyebrows. Was she laughing inside? Her eyes sparkled, but she looked cool and still, like always.

I reached to tug my hair before I remembered it was back up in a ballerina bun. "Is there anything I can do? Is it too late for me to try for the Big League?"

"Yes and no. It's not."

Confused, I pushed my glasses up, then squinted at her. Her answers didn't make sense.

"Yes, there's something we can do," she explained. "No, it's not too late for you to try to get into the Big League." Her face remained serious, but now I definitely saw a smile creeping from her eyes to her cheeks.

I gasped, inhaling joy and nervousness all jumbled together. It felt scary but exciting. Like when you fly a little too high on the swing, but you don't really wanna come down.

"I didn't want to get your hopes up, so I didn't say anything," she said. "On Friday after school I spoke to the principal. It's not easy, what you have to do."

I held my breath, waiting for the bad news.

"You'll have to go to each teacher one by one. Make the case for why we should do another round."

The air escaped me, like a deflated balloon. Jitters replaced all the joy.

"*I* have to do it?" I stretched the word *I* till it was nearly two syllables long.

"Yes, yoouuu," she said. "Some students might feel it's unfair. You missed it, even if you had a good reason. So figure out a plan. But you can't drag your feet. The Big League is Friday. You have until *Wednesday* to convince the teachers, and their top players, to allow a do-over. Got it?"

"Yes, ma'am, I got it," I said quietly. Eight days left. I turned around, my eyes on the floor. I didn't feel like I had it at all. The courage. The confidence. How would I pull this off?

✫

At lunch I explained everything to Marquez, Rashida, and Shelby. The idea of talking to every teacher and asking for something special terrified me. But at the same time I was sick of feeling that way. I needed to do more of this heart-training thing. We agreed to brainstorm for homework and nail down our plan at school tomorrow.

Tomorrow would also be a big day for the chicks: Hatch Day. We clapped when Ms. W. announced the news. As always, she projected a picture. "By tonight, the chicks will be nearly the size of the eggshell. The beak is twisted under her wing," she said, pointing out the details in the picture so we could sketch it in our journals. "She should be ready to take her first breath inside the egg."

She reminded us that the humidity in the incubator will keep the membranes moist so the chicks can break through it. If their membranes get too dry, the chicks might just suffocate and die.

We all gasped, horrified at the thought.

"See?" Ms. W. said, pointing to the condensation inside the dome.

"That's a lot of water," said Marquez. "Will it rain?"

We laughed, but when we settled down, I heard something.

"What's that sound?" I blurted out without even thinking.

"What sound?" asked William. "Are you hearing things now?"

Rashida rolled her eyes at him so hard he blushed.

"Anyway," said Rashida, leaning toward the incubator, "she's right. I hear it, too." Everyone looked at Rashida. "It's coming from over there." She pointed. All eyes followed her finger, but no one moved. No one except Marquez, who motioned for me to go take a look.

It would be so easy for anyone else to walk over there. *Just do it*, I said to myself. Maybe this was heart training. I took a deep breath and pushed my shoulders back and stood up. *Don't trip*, I warned myself.

Ms. W. didn't tell me to sit down. No one said anything. But the silence turned out to be the best thing. There was no denying it now.

"It's the chicks!" I said, all fear melting away. I darted the last few steps to the incubator and leaned closer. "Someone's peeping! They're alive!" I shouted.

I heard chairs squeaking and sliding and Ms. W. warning everyone to be quiet and calm and not trip over each other.

Suddenly my classmates surrounded me. Everyone tried to poke their way beside me. I did not duck away or shrink or blend in. I kept my spot. Right in the middle. I leaned in and cheeped at the nearest egg. She heard me! She cheeped back.

Tomorrow they hatch.

CHAPTER TWENTY-NINE
Late Bloomer

This morning's April showers meant we all got a little soggy waiting at the bus stop. By the time I walked into class, Rashida was standing watch at the incubator. With her finger up to her mouth she waved us over, grinning so big. I've never seen so many teeth in her mouth.

"Look!" she mouthed dramatically, and then she cupped her ear, telling us to listen, too.

Two of the eggs had holes, and a couple of the others were peeping!

Everyone in the room crowded around to coo and giggle and point. We examined our favorites. Even now, we knew we couldn't officially count them. But we did unofficial counts.

"Ladies, gentlemen, everyone—let's give the chicks some breathing room," said Ms. W. over our heads. "It may take a few hours," she said. "They get that nice air from outside, and then they take a nap."

She waved us away from the incubator and back to

unpacking for the day. She told us it might take them all day or longer to finish hatching. We should be patient and not bother them.

I had to admit, I felt disappointed mine had shown no signs of life yet. *I guess she's a late bloomer,* I thought.

I wonder if she will hatch.

I think so.

I hope so, anyway.

✭

The chicks were exciting, but I had another important thing to worry about—Mind Bender. At lunch we whispered about the plan. We needed to figure out how to convince the fifth grade teachers and the other players to redo the round. And we had to hope that Kyle would be okay competing again for his own spot.

Shelby took notes.

By recess, the weather had cleared up. It wasn't dry enough for races or dodgeball, but you could still jump rope and shoot hoops and stand around with friends.

"Let's review our strategy one more time," said Rashida. She flashed an index card. She had written all the scores by round. My name was at the bottom of Round 2.

"Rashida is number one," said Shelby. "By a lot! Wow."

Marquez looked over her shoulder. "Kyle is second place, but he's pretty far back. And look, he was only barely ahead of third and fourth. It's almost a three-way tie."

"Even though you missed a round, Jillian, your last place is pretty respectable," Shelby joked. Everyone laughed. She had a point.

We fought over the details and how to present everything to the teachers. But by the end we worked out all the important stuff.

"All right! One more time," announced Shelby, reading from her notes.

THE PLAN
1. EXPLAIN WHY YOU WERE ABSENT — SHOW THE EXCUSE
2. ASK FOR A DO-OVER WITH THE TOP 5 — YOU'RE NUMBER 5
3. ASK THE LIBRARIAN TO HOST MIND BENDER REDO DURING LUNCH OR RECESS
4. USE TOP SCORES FOR ALL PLAYERS TO SEE WHO ADVANCES

"So do we just make a big presentation to all the fifth grade teachers at once?" she asked.

"No!" shouted Rashida and Marquez together.

"Nah," said Marquez. "We ask Ms. Dub to write a note, so we're official and stuff. We're not just saying she *said* it's okay."

"Exactly. We go to them one by one," said Rashida. "Plus

we have to ask Mr. Kline if he's available. Librarians are very busy people."

We all nodded.

We decided to kick off the plan in the morning. We'd ask our parents to bring us early instead of riding the bus.

"Gotta get up with the chickens, like my grandma says." Marquez smiled.

"When did you get to be so good at planning?" asked Rashida.

"Je suis excellent! It's all up here—" He tapped his temple.

We all shook our heads.

He continued, amped now. "Jillian, you ask Ms. Dub for the note. We'll come around with you in the morning, but *you* gotta do all the talking."

"I agree." Rashida nodded.

Then Shelby wanted to know what we were wearing. We all stared at her.

"I mean, we're a team, right? Shouldn't we look like it?" she asked.

On a normal Wednesday, the last thing I'd want to do is dress like everyone else. But she had a point. It's different when we're being a *team* instead of just doing what everyone else does. I guess we all agreed because pretty soon we were all nodding.

"Does everyone have blue jeans?" I asked. "I really, really don't wanna wear beige."

"Okay—and white shirts?" said Shelby "We all have that, right?"

Rashida suggested we wear ponytails.

Marquez gave her a look. "I'm not wearing a ponytail," he said. We all laughed.

I looked around at everyone. Up until these past few days, Marquez was the only person in class I called my friend. This whole thing started because of Rashida, and here she was, one of the biggest champions on my side.

I never cry in public (except that one time the other day). But I have to admit, after planning everything with them, I felt like crying. The good kind. Not nervous. Not sad. No throat thick with envy. Just really glad.

"Thanks, you guys," I said. I made myself look at them, not at the ground. "Thanks for helping me. It means a lot."

"That's what friends are for!" Shelby winked. Or she tried to. She closed both eyes, instead of just one.

✫

When I got home, I thought it would be fun to make something for the team. It wouldn't take much time to make a few hair ties by hand. They'd add a little splash of color to our ponytails. Plus, Grammy said creating something—anything—was special.

I dug through my yarn baskets to see what colors I had. I plopped out some red, of course, a yellow one and a silvery white. I got to work on the first one when I saw the frayed triangle paper. "Oh," I said out loud, finally remembering Grammy telling me about Nit when I was little.

I sat in her lap while she weaved, playing with scrap yarn the color of jewels—aqua, green, and purple. She told me about the goddess Nit—a wise, weaving warrior. Told me I was just like her. I feel okay about the wise and weaving part. Warrior? Not yet.

CHAPTER THIRTY
Early Birds

Daddy drove me to school early the next morning. Mama's lupus flare had almost passed, and he wanted her to get as much sleep as she could. When I arrived, I found Shelby already waiting in the cafeteria. She had told Ms. Jenkins, one of the grownups on cafeteria duty, why we were there early. Ms. Jenkins called our teacher and confirmed what we were up to. I hadn't thought about all that stuff, but Shelby's mom is an organizer. She says kids have to tell advocates all the details if you want a smooth path.

It wasn't long before Marquez and Rashida walked up to us.

"You ready?" asked Marquez.

I took a deep breath and made a slurping sound.

"What's that?" asked Rashida, wrinkling her forehead.

"Me, sucking in my gut."

"Like the chicks?" Marquez frowned. "Yuck!"

I nodded, impressed he got it so fast. "I'm nervous," I

admitted. "I'm glad y'all are here." I flashed my index cards. I had written down what I wanted to say, so I wouldn't forget or stutter too much. I got boos and thumbs-downs. No one liked that idea. They wanted me to just tell the truth and be myself. Easy for them to say.

"Think of something funny, remember?" said Rashida.

I stared at her. She looked elegant. Standing tall and graceful even in her T-shirt and jeans. Calm, cool, and collected. Like always. I tried to push down the feeling of jealousy that crept into my throat. I swallowed. Hard. I shoved my notes into my back pocket. Or tried to. They wouldn't fit.

"Oh yeah," I said, remembering. I reached into my pocket and pulled out four red and yellow ribbons. "I weaved these last night!"

Rashida and Shelby gasped, and each pulled one from my outstretched palm. Marquez saw mine and the one extra. He smiled his big, dimply grin.

"I told you, I'm not wearing a ponytail."

"I know, but I felt funny leaving you out. We said we're a team, right?"

"Here, hold out your arm," said Rashida. "Let's say it's a friendship bracelet. You can wear that, can't you?"

"Yeah, I guess. Why not?" He shrugged and let Rashida tie it around his wrist.

Shelby wanted to wear hers as a bracelet, too. Soon we all had them on.

We reviewed the plan one more time and got permission from Ms. Jenkins to head to the fifth grade hall. On the way, we debated which teacher to see first. We still hadn't figured that part out.

"Let's ask Ms. W.," said Rashida. "We have to get her note anyway. She might have some advice."

We knocked on the door to our classroom, and Ms. W. greeted us in the hallway with a big smile.

"Look at my little chickadees! All dressed alike . . ." She laughed, giving us all high-fives. "Is this your handiwork, Jillian?" she asked, pointing to our bracelets.

I blushed and nodded yes.

"I like," she said, giving me a thumbs-up.

We explained our dilemma. She nodded and wrote down the fifth grade teachers in the order she thought we should visit.

"Leave your bookbags here," she said, handing over the list and her letter. "I'll put them on your desks."

We plopped them by the classroom door and set off.

☆

First up, Mrs. Fueyo. Shelby knocked, even though the door was open. The teacher welcomed us, looking curious but friendly.

I couldn't think of anything funny to calm myself down. I couldn't think of anything at all. We stood there until Marquez elbowed me and announced, "This is Jillian. And we're here about Mind Bender?"

She seemed to know exactly who we were then. Her smile brightened as she waited. Apparently Ms. W. wasn't the only teacher who knew how to use Wait Time.

Rashida cleared her throat, and that was my cue.

"I'm Jillian," I said to the teacher's knees, my heartbeat drumming away. "And I . . . My mom . . . I mean . . . I had a fair shot at being one of the finalists. But I missed the round."

I saw Shelby near me, nodding hard. Not just her head, but her whole body shook. I gulped and forced myself to look up. I tried again with a little more volume.

"My mother was in the hospital, and I missed school that day. We . . ." I ran out of steam. I reached back, wanting my notes from my back pocket. Rashida, seeing what I was up to, jumped in. "I'm Rashida — the reigning champion."

"Oh, I remember you from last year," said Mrs. Fueyo, nodding. "And don't you have a twin sister? Where is she?"

"We aren't twins, but we do look a lot alike."

"Is she doing the Mind Bender, too?"

"No, ma'am. She's not into competitions. Just me. Anyway, we have an idea!"

Rashida turned to me then. Everyone did, their eyebrows stretching way up, telling me to get on with it.

I exhaled and started again.

"Can we please redo the round? Everyone can use their best score to see who wins."

Shelby nodded at me to keep going.

I stood a little taller. "We can redo it if all the fifth grade teachers and players agree. Maybe Kyle won't mind."

Shelby handed her the note then. Ms. W.'s official stamp of approval. Mrs. Fueyo glanced at it, nodding.

"Well, it's all fine with me. Believe it or not, I think Kyle would agree. He said you were a pretty tough cookie, Rashida. And we've heard good things about you, too, Jillian." She smiled at me. I didn't duck, but I wanted to. "I'll run it by Kyle, and I'll let Ms. Warren know." She handed the note back.

We said thank you and rushed into the hall. They were laughing, but I collapsed on the wall.

Shelby spoke first. "That wasn't too bad, was it?"

"One down, three to go!" said Rashida.

I stared at them. I wanted to relax and smile, too. All I could think was that I had to go do that whole thing all over again. My heart thumped so hard. And I could barely swallow.

"Momentum!" yelled Marquez. "Let's go before you get nervous again."

I almost laughed at that one. *Too late,* I thought.

And off we went.

None of the teachers seemed surprised to see us, and at

least two of them laughed, like they were in on a joke. Every-one said they'd confirm with Ms. W. after their contestant arrived.

I have to admit, the last one was the easiest. After three other conversations, I knew what to expect. Still, I was exhausted by the time we returned to our class. All I wanted to do was take a nap.

But the excitement was starting. Chicks! No wonder Ms. W. had us leave our stuff outside. She had a surprise!

Some of the chickens had hatched overnight and early this morning. They were still damp and stumbling around. One of them looked pooped, completely stretched out but breathing (we checked). We pushed each other until every-one mushed in to watch. Ms. W. laughed and took pictures of us cooing and peeping at the chicks. We marveled until the morning announcements came on, when we finally had to go sit down and start the day.

Everyone chattered about the chicks. I smiled, but I couldn't really hear anyone over the voices in my head. All morning I replayed the conversations with the teachers. I sounded so goofy. My cheeks got hot every time I remem-bered a mistake or thought of a better way to say something. I kept hearing myself mess up, over and over again. I couldn't concentrate on anything else, couldn't turn off the recording in my head.

Finally it was time for lunch.

Since fifth grade girls dress alike every day, no one really noticed that we were the four Musketeers. No one except William, who asked quite loudly at lunch, "Did I miss the memo?"

We all looked at him, but no one said anything.

"You're all dressed alike. Did you plan it?"

He pointed at Marquez's wrist. At all our wrists. "And what's that?" He sounded snippy as usual. But when I looked at him, I saw something different. Loneliness.

"We did plan it," explained Rashida. "We had to do a team presentation this morning before school."

"Oh," he said. "How was it?"

He had eyes only for Rashida, like he really *needed* to believe her. Like he felt left out. Hurt.

"I think it went okay. We'll find out later today."

After lunch, William cut in front of me.

"Hey Weaver—" He turned to face me. "What's it like to be kicked out of Mind Bender? I told you Rashida would win."

I wanted to say something, but this time it wasn't fear or anger that kept me from talking. I could still see the hurt. Done taunting me, he faced front as our line filed out.

"They're friendship bracelets. I can make you one, too," I said to his back.

He flinched, but gave no other hint that he heard me. And that was that.

I asked Marquez about William at recess. Why he was so mean sometimes. Why he seemed so down.

"Remember we said everyone has a battle?"

I nodded.

He didn't explain. I didn't expect Marquez to take William's side, but it seemed he knew something I didn't. What if William was trying to be seen? Or just be himself? And didn't know who that was yet? He was wrong to be mean to me, but what if there was more to it?

"Over here, Jillian." Ms. W.'s voice snapped me back to reality. She and the rest of the team were waving to get my attention.

She cleared her throat before springing the news. "Everyone agreed to a redo!"

"Yay!" We cheered and gave high-fives all around.

"Highest points wins. We'll do a tiebreaker if we get to the end and we need it."

"When?" asked Marquez.

"Tomorrow during recess. And they agreed, if anyone is absent, they will use the points they already have. Including you, Jillian." She stared at me. "Understand?"

Everyone looked at me. I looked at the ground instead. "Yes, ma'am," I said to my feet.

She lifted my chin. "Keep your head up, Jillian. Just be yourself. Got it?"

"Got it."

I think so.

I hope so, anyway.

✬

For the rest of the day, we watched the chicks get fluffy in the warm air. They took naps on top of each other—little golden pillows. So cute.

Five chicks are out. Mine isn't, but I can tell she is dancing inside. My egg actually rocked back and forth a little! Maybe she knows how to jump rope.

Before we left, some of the baby chicks stood over the unhatched eggs, peeping. Ms. W. said they were telling the others they could do it, too.

Come on little chicken, come on!

✬

When I came down for dinner, I was surprised to see Mama in the kitchen, ladling soup.

"You're up? You cooked?"

"Just spreading my wings a little bit. Tired of being *cooped* up in my room. Get it?"

"*Ba dum tss,*" said Daddy, playing an invisible drum set.

"Oh my gosh." I buried my face in my hands.

"I'm feeling good, so I just wanted to make something. Grilled cheese sandwiches and tomato soup. Okay?"

"Okay!" I kissed her cheek, happy to see her up and about. "Guess what?"

"Chicken butt," she said.

194

"Mama!" I laughed.

She shrugged.

"You're on a roll, babe," said Daddy.

"The chicks! They started to hatch."

"See?" she said. "I was right!"

I hid my face again. I looked up to see her standing right beside me.

"Can you two handle the kitchen?" she asked.

"Feeling okay?" Daddy asked, reaching for her.

"Yes! Doc says to quit while I'm ahead. I'm going to rest before I have too much fun."

Daddy and I nodded, and she kissed us both good night.

CHAPTER THIRTY-ONE
Make a Peep

Two eggs remain unhatched. Mine and Scottie's is one of them. Of course. But I'm excited because she's going to make it. She has unzipped. She's almost free!

The other one still hasn't made a move. No pip. No peeps. That one belongs to Shelby and Marquez. Marquez has a brave face, but Shelby looks sadder every hour it doesn't hatch. Ms. W. says it's too early to give up.

"Look"—I pointed—"they're peeping at it. The baby chicks are telling her she can do it. They know she's in there."

Shelby nodded. Her eyes were wet, but she didn't cry.

I pushed my glasses up my nose and nodded back at her. "The chickens know," I said. I felt sure about that.

I didn't feel as sure about the Mind Bender. Today is the do-over round. I know what I need to know. But I still haven't figured out how to relax. How to be calm, cool, and collected. Maybe someone will peep at me and tell me I can do it.

It was a perfect April afternoon. Where sunshine warms goose-bumpy skin, cold from the indoor air conditioning. Clear skies with soft honeysuckle breezes. So pretty, the grownups decided to host the Mind Bender do-over outside.

There we were in the "competition area," a small set of bleachers facing the playground. Rashida, Ryan, Jared, Kyle, and I sat in a row. Besides Rashida, who would be the last person standing?

After the first question, I had no idea. I heard it. I knew the answer. But like before, the words remained trapped. I could see them, but could not pull them from my head and out of my mouth.

I sighed and reminded myself to pull my shoulders back and sit up straight. *You can do it, Jilly,* I thought. *You are a wise, weaving warrior. You can do it!*

Most kids ignored us. Almost no one wanted to waste the sunshine, hanging around watching kids answer questions. My team did, though. Marquez and Shelby sat in the grass. So did a couple more from the other classes.

Shelby had a big smile when we began. She looked worried by the second question. Shrinking smile, dimming eyes, and hands folded in prayer position under her chin. Marquez held steady. Game face. I tried to block them out and focus on the next question, when out of nowhere, William appeared.

Arms folded across his chest, he yelled. At me! "Stop being such a chicken, Weaver!"

It was so outrageous. Mr. Kline turned to shush him. William looked mad—at me! Like I was somehow letting *him* down. I got hot. Anger jumped from my toes to my face, and I felt prickly with sweat. *Stop being such a chicken, Weaver!* I repeated it to myself. And just as fast as the heat flared up, the silliest thing came to mind.

Peck.

I pecked my head at him. Just like a chicken. Just like that day when we knew the future chicks were growing their beaks. *Peck.*

Marquez and Shelby burst out laughing. William smirked. The other students sorta giggled. They were hatching chicks in their classes, too, so maybe they understood. But I guess that's what I needed. Something silly to lift my spirits and break the shell. Something to help me pip.

"Are we ready?" asked Mr. Kline to settle us down.

Everyone said some version of "Yes, sir," and the round resumed until we had our top two.

Chickens and Champions

They're out. All of them. Every single chick.

Ms. W. said the last one pipped after we left for the day. She must've unzipped and pushed sometime last night.

The new one was still a little damp this morning, but the others are dry and fluffy and cute. We worried that they were hungry, but Ms. W. reminded us that that's what the yolk was for—keeping them alive and well the first couple of days. She will give the newest ones a little more time to dry out, so they don't get cold and shiver to death (it happens!). Then they'll all move to their new home for real food and water and a little freedom.

The best part? WE COUNTED THEM! And we named them, too.

We had a big ceremony. Even William pointed and laughed. It wasn't a Dirty Dozen, but it *was* a Perfect Ten. Marquez introduced them, of course.

We all cheered. And unless the other teachers have more chicks hatching that we don't know about, Ms. W. has the most.

Again.

☆

After we counted the chicks, it was time to crown the champion. All the upper grade classes were invited to attend the Mind Bender Big League in the school cafeteria. It has a stage, with heavy red curtains, for special events. There are even a few colored lights in the ceiling. The grownups sometimes call it the cafetorium.

There were six finalists. Two each from third, fourth, and fifth grades. Representing fifth grade? Rashida, ~~my foe,~~ my worthy adversary, my friend.

And me.

She was the favorite to win. I had a decent chance at second. A spunky fourth-grader was third, and then the others. Rashida had been a spunky fourth-grader when she won the whole thing last year, so she was proof this was anybody's game.

The curtains were pulled back, revealing a long table and chairs for all the finalists. A matching red cloth covered the table, like a fancy Thanksgiving dinner. A microphone, a small buzzer, and a printed name tent sat in front of each chair. I saw scraps of paper and pencils, too. There were even little cups of water! This was official.

I looked to my left and saw William biting and chewing his fingernails. I tapped him on the shoulder, then held out a friendship bracelet. He looked at me, eyes wide with surprise. He hesitated, then took it, like he thought I might snatch it away. Neither of us said anything after that.

I patted my hair—two Afro puffs, my power puffs—then balled up all my nervous energy into tight fists. Marquez gave me a look, like he didn't know if he wanted to tell a joke or say something serious. He split the difference. Told me I'm not a chicken after all, maybe just an egghead. That did it. I wanted to cry because it was sweet—and laugh because it was funny. I split the difference, too. I smiled with watery eyes, then blinked them dry again.

Ms. W. called my name and pointed to the front. I could barely hear directions over my heartbeat. I followed Rashida and the other finalists to line up beside the stage. I wanted to fly away. I also wanted to win.

The assistant principal called us to find our seats. Our name tents were in alphabetical order.

I felt numb, like only part of me was inside my body. The part keeping me awake and breathing. The thinking/feeling part had disappeared. I chewed my tongue, but I couldn't feel it. Whoever or whatever took my thinking and feeling also took my memory. I tried to remember something. Anything.

When I sat down, I wanted to drink that water, but I was

afraid my hands would shake too much and everyone would see. And laugh.

I told myself not to faint. I looked out, and Marquez flashed me a smile and a thumbs-up. Then, in a quiet moment, as short as Ms. W.'s hair, he sneezed. I was the only one who heard "JTRA."

"Bless you," said everyone nearby.

Suddenly I saw the eggs in my mind. Day twenty or so, when you can hear some of them start to peep. Even though they are still inside, they need air. They use that egg tooth and peck a hole in the air cell so they can breathe. And when they are finally ready, they pip that shell.

I closed my eyes and pictured myself inside the oval. Balled up, ready for air. In my imagination I pecked and broke through the air cell. Then I pipped the shell.

It worked. I could breathe. Maybe I wouldn't die after all.

I heard James, a fourth-grader, snicker on my left. I guess he saw me pip. But I didn't care. That little bit of air wouldn't be enough for the whole tournament, but it was enough for now.

Mr. Kline and Mrs. Daniel took their seats in front of the stage. Their table also had mics and a tablet. They'd award points and tally scores electronically. But the math coach would also tally by hand, just in case. The assistant principal tapped her mic, and the competition began.

We started with the warm-up round. I tried to listen to

everyone else's category. To their questions and answers. But it was like hearing Charlie Brown's teacher. I couldn't understand anything. *What would help me get free?* I asked myself. A math question. *The kind Rashida beat me on. No, the kind I "let" her beat me on,* I reminded myself. I shifted in my seat. *I'm smart. I'm a warrior. I can do this.* Pip.

No one picks math problems. There's too much that can go wrong. If it's a word problem, you can miss steps. You can miscalculate. You can misunderstand the question. All questions have time limits, and judges repeat them only once.

"Jillian," said Mr. Kline.

"Math?" My answer was a question. Like I wasn't sure. Who can be sure? I saw my classmates fidgeting. I saw a flash of metal from Marquez's braces. He smiled. I pushed my glasses on my nose and said it louder. "Math."

Pip.

No talking. No talking was allowed from the audience, but I heard them. Everyone had something to say. Mostly versions of *wow.* I held my pencil in shaky fingers and stared at Mr. Kline.

"What is the next number in this pattern," he began, "and what is the rule? 1, 1, 2, 3, 5, 8."

I couldn't believe my luck. I'd know this pattern anywhere. *Say it say it say it!*

I took a breath. *Say it say it. Come on, say it.*

"Thirteen," I mustered. My voice sounded funny. Like it

belonged to someone else. I cleared my throat. I had to hurry before I ran out of time.

"Add the two previous numbers to get the next one." I said as fast as I could. "So, five plus eight equals thirteen." I forgot to lean away from the mic. My loud exhale filled the cafeteria.

I heard a few giggles, but I pushed them away. *Stop worrying about what everyone else thinks,* I heard Grammy say.

"Correct," said Mr. Kline.

My mouth was dry, and I was still too nervous to drink water, or make out James's question, but feeling came back into my body then. I sat up straight, with that imaginary dictionary on my head, and tried to swallow.

I twisted my friendship bracelet for good luck. That's when I noticed Rashida's wrist. She had hers on, too! I smiled to myself and took another breath before the Fair and Square round.

Sixty questions. All subjects, all grades. I have to admit, once I relaxed, I did okay. I guessed Rashida was in the lead but I didn't mind. I didn't have to work so hard to pull answers out of my mouth. And after a while I even thought it was fun.

Unzip.

"Okay, everyone. Final question."

I told myself to remain calm. My heart didn't get the

message, but I had made up my mind. I had my power puffs, my glasses, and my magic bracelet. All I could do was my best.

"If H is equal to 10, and T is half of M, how can MATH be 42, TEAM be 40, and MEET be 37?"

My mouth fell open. The cafeteria buzzed as everyone chuckled and chatted in shock. The assistant principal waved wildly to quiet everyone down. I tried not to see what anyone else on stage did.

Focus, Jillian. I thought. *You can do this.*

I waited for Mr. Kline to repeat himself and then wrote the problem as fast as I could. I made myself write neatly. Now was not the time to write chicken scratch and be unable to read it.

The 37 meant there would be an odd number in the solution. And just like that, I could see the way to the answer.

I finished working the problem as others scribbled. I laid my pencil on the table with no fanfare. I floated my hand toward the buzzer while everyone watched. But they weren't watching me, they were watching Rashida. Because they knew she was going to win. Again.

Through my red glasses and Ms. W.'s golden ones, my eyes locked on hers. I swallowed, then hit the buzzer. The whole room inhaled at once.

In the stillness that followed, I put my face down, but I

promised myself I would not disappear. I would not become invisible.

"Jillian?" Mr. Kline acknowledged me.

I leaned into the mic, staring only at my paper. My voice shook as I read the answer, "M equals 14, A equals 11, T equals 7, H equals 10, E equals 8."

Silence. The only time a cafeteria is this quiet is when it's empty. I held my breath with everyone else and prayed, again, that I wouldn't pass out.

"That is correct."

A few cheers and shocked gasps flew around the cafeteria, but everyone waited for the real news. Mrs. Daniel and Mr. Kline bent their heads together to tally and double-check the scores. Then Mr. Kline cleared his throat for the big announcement.

CHAPTER THIRTY-THREE
Today I Was Brave

"Congratulations, Jillian. You are this year's Mind Bender champion!"

I replayed Mr. Kline's announcement in my head over and over on our way back to the classroom, but I couldn't believe it. My classmates patted my back and joked about their favorite parts of the competition. I smiled, but I couldn't really hear them.

My team, my friends, gathered around me to say congratulations one more time. Prim and proper Rashida, who speaks crisply and glides with her shiny twists, who dances while she jumps, and laughs from her belly, hugged me.

"I always knew you could do it," she said, smiling a big smile.

"Me, too," said Marquez.

"Me, three," Shelby chimed in.

"Yeah, yeah," said William. "When she stopped being such a chicken, I figured she had half a shot."

We had a good laugh at that.

"Thanks, Weaver," he said, quiet enough so only I heard. He pointed to his wrist, flashing me the red and gold friendship bracelet I'd made for him. Then he faded back to his seat while we packed up to go home.

Ms. W. waved me over to her desk, where she stood smiling. Today she wore rainbow-colored rhombus earrings. They sparkled as she leaned close to me. She whispered, "I know a girl who once said 'everyone knows who'll win.'"

I blushed, but I didn't say anything.

"The toughest battle, the most important one, is *always* the one inside, Jillian."

I nodded.

Then she tapped the First Place medal around my neck. "Never count yourself out. Got it?"

I laughed, "Yes, ma'am, I got it."

It started to sink in then. I really did it. I was the Mind Bender champion! I skipped to the bus, wondering if I would explode from all the skipping my heart was doing, too.

On the bus, a few kids gave me high-fives and pointed at my medal. In my head I heard myself screaming at everyone *CAN YOU BELIEVE WHAT HAPPENED? I WON!* In real life, I smiled and nodded but mostly sat still. I held in all that joy and disbelief. For now, anyway.

Marquez started a round of yo mama jokes, and things were the same as always.

I got off at my stop and waved goodbye to everyone. I heard the word *winner* drift my way, but I pretended not to notice.

I speed-walked the last bit home, laughing to myself. My hand shook as I pushed the key into the lock and barged into the house. Mama had left a snack and a note saying she'd be right back. I ran to my room and shut the door.

I did it! I really did it, I thought. *I wasn't invisible. I wasn't a copycat, or a chicken. I was Just Jillian! Just like Grammy wanted. Just like I wanted, too.*

And even though nobody was home, I took off my red glasses, covered my head with my pillow, and screamed with joy, then cried myself into a happy sleep.

☆

I woke up to Daddy calling my name. I must've napped a long time, because the house already smelled yummy. I snatched off my medal and stuffed it into my back pocket, then dashed to the kitchen to see bright colors and bright smiles.

"What's going on?" I asked, shocked to see red, yellow, and aqua balloons all around the kitchen.

"Today was the big day, right? It's a celebration!" said Daddy.

"I didn't even tell you what happened," I said, my surprise fading to giggles.

"Oh, right. So . . . how'd it go?" asked Daddy, hiding his eyes dramatically, awaiting the news.

"You promise not to overreact?"

"No matter what," said Mama, "you're a winner, Jilly Bean."

"Mama," I said, sliding the medal from my back pocket but keeping it behind my back.

"You mastered your mind," Daddy said. "You did not let your mind master you."

"Daddy!" I huffed and turned away from them. I straightened out the medal, slipped it over my head, and turned back around in one smooth move. If I do say so myself.

I cleared my throat. "You're looking at the Mae Jemison Elementary MIND BENDER CHAMPION!"

Cheers and claps all around.

"See?" said Daddy. "This definitely calls for a celebration. Let's eat!" He pointed to the table, already set with turkey burgers and sweet potato fries.

"Is this what I think it is?" I grabbed one of the tall glasses of red juice and drank a big gulp. "Cherry limeade! Grammy's favorite! Aww. Thank you!"

"Overreacting?" asked Daddy, his eyes twinkling.

I shook my head no.

"Underreacting?" asked Mama, smiling.

"No!" I laughed. "Everything is perfect. It's just right."

CHAPTER THIRTY-FOUR
Free as a Bird

It's the last day of April. The chickens are escaping today. I'm sad, but they shouldn't be in cages. "They need to roam and roost," said Ms. W. "Not listen to Marquez make jokes."

If you could see blushing on dark brown cheeks, we saw it today.

Shelby asked why the last one out was so late to hatch.

Ms. W. said she wasn't late at all. "Chickens, just like plants and people, grow when they're ready." She joked that some of us didn't show up exactly when our parents thought we would. We laughed about that.

Marquez said he was proud of me. Called me a true champion. That's the biggest compliment I've ever gotten. I might even believe it now.

I asked Marquez about his training. The spring cleaning. His dad.

"It's cool," he said. "I needed him to get that me and Moms and sis are good."

"He got it?"

He nodded his head, "Yeah. He'll always be my dad. And Moms said we can see him whenever we want."

"What about his stuff?"

"He took most of it this weekend! I helped. Moms is laughing again. Sis is getting a kitten soon. Everything is cool," he said, smiling a real smile. Braces and dimples and all.

I smiled back. Then we packed up to go home.

Tomorrow is May Day. The one-year anniversary of Grammy's leaving us. I have surprises! A new belt for Mama and a guitar strap for Daddy. I weaved them both with ruby red yarn. I also decorated that old scrap of paper I found. The one six-year-old me wrote about the goddess Nit. I'm gonna hang it right beside my loom, so I can remember that I'm a wise, weaving warrior, just like Grammy said.

The bell rang, and Ms. W. waved goodbye.

Rashida glided over to me. "You're always smiling at him. Why?" she asked, pointing at Marquez.

"I dunno. He sees me. The real me. Just Jillian."

She nodded, like she understood.

"And you know what?"

"What?" she asked.

"I see the real me now, too."

Acknowledgments

As a little girl attending Continental Colony Elementary School in Atlanta, Georgia, I wrote three books. They were each handmade, stitched and bound, covered with construction paper shapes and markered titles.

Thanks to my mother, I still have two of those books. They are fading and falling apart, but on those pages, you can still read the dreams of a child. I told of my plans to keep writing, and to someday become a children's author like Judy Blume.

It's been more than thirty-five years since then. The journey from that dream to this debut reality was a circuitous one, and I am thankful for the many people who helped me take steps along the path.

I'm grateful to Tayari Jones, whose encouragement that people who work every day have stories to tell, too, helped me be gentle with myself when the writing was slow going.

Tayari has spent many years penning beautiful books and making the writing life accessible. Thank you for that.

Thank you to Zetta Elliott and Sista Docta Alexis Pauline Gumbs, who show by example what creativity and trailblazing look like in action. Also to Deesha Philyaw and Lisa Lewis Tyre for your encouragement. It was early and genuine, and I held it top of mind for every step of this journey.

To People of Color in Publishing, thank you for the life-changing opportunity to pair with a great mentor, Christina Soontornvat. Christina, thank you so much for your generosity, wisdom, and kindness. I appreciate you!

Thank you to Upstart Crow Literary, especially my agent, Danielle Chiotti. Danielle, thank you for everything, and in particular for your editorial eye, your savvy, and your warmth.

A million thanks to my editor, Margaret Raymo, for seeing Jillian through loving eyes. Even though Jillian is afraid of the spotlight, you made sure she could shine. And thank you to everyone at Team Versify, including Kwame Alexander and Erika Turner, for believing in the manuscript's potential and helping to make publication a reality. I also deeply appreciate the copyeditor, Maxine Bartow, cover artist, Kitt Thomas, and jacket designer, Mary Claire Cruz. Where would Jillian be without your care and conscientiousness? And no one would have the chance to meet Jillian if it weren't for Lisa DiSarro, Tara Shanahan, and Zoe Del Mar.

I appreciate Forsyth County Public Library's critique group members for reading early pages, and the Next Level Writing Group for fostering a supportive writing community. And thanks to Chris Negron, a member of both, who offered great feedback on the completed manuscript. More than that, Chris, you were always ready to share a helpful response to my tweets, texts, and emails. Thank you for that.

To Alexis, my first beta reader, thank you so much for reading and sharing your insights.

To Samuel F. Reynolds, thanks for your answers to my quirky questions, and for always reminding me of the books inside.

Thank you to my BFF and husband, Phillip, aka Blue, for being a great partner and listener, and for making sure I had a "room of my own."

I'm sending love and gratitude to my parents, Victoria and Edisel Collier. They passed away many moons ago, but they are never far.

And thanks to all my ancestors, family, friends, and sorors. There are far too many to name, but I love and appreciate you all.

Every word on paper becomes a tiny step forward. Here's to the next one.